Backcourt Ace

The Chip Hilton Sports Series

For more information on
Coach Clair Bee and **Chip Hilton**
please visit us at
www.chiphilton.com

Chip Hilton Sports Series

#19

Backcourt Ace

Coach Clair Bee

Foreword by Dr. Rogers McAvoy

Updated by Randall and Cynthia Bee Farley

BROADMAN
&HOLMAN
PUBLISHERS

Nashville, Tennessee

0-8054-2098-3

Published by Broadman & Holman Publishers,
Nashville, Tennessee

Subject Heading: BASKETBALL—FICTION / YOUTH
Library of Congress Card Catalog Number: 00-068883

Library of Congress Cataloging-in-Publication Data
Bee, Clair, 1900–83
      Backcourt ace / Clair Bee ; updated by Randall and
Cynthia Bee Farley ; foreword by Rogers McAvoy.
      p. cm. — (Chip Hilton sports series ; #19)
      Summary: Chip Hilton and his teammates doubt that even
Chip's scoring prowess will be enough to help State University win
the Holiday Invitational Tournament, but a seven-foot-tall junior
might, so they hope to find a way to get him to play for their team.
      ISBN 0-8054-2098-3 (pb)
      [1. Basketball—Fiction.] I. Farley, Randall K., 1952– .
II. Farley, Cynthia Bee, 1952– . III. Title.

PZ7.B38196 Bae   2001
[Fic]—dc21   00-068883

1 2 3 4 5 6 7 8 9 10 05 04 03 02 01

John Kahabka

COACH CLAIR BEE, 1961

Paddy Clark

Conservationist, Forester, Great Fishing Guide—
and a True New Zealand Legend

RANDY AND CINDY FARLEY, 2001

Contents

Afterword by Clark Power, University of Notre Dame

Foreword

CLAIR BEE grew up in the small town of Grafton, West Virginia. His ancestral history reaches back through several generations of ministers who helped establish the Seventh Day Baptist Church in the area. From these two sources, the small town and religious family background, Clair Bee acquired a set of values that sustained him through his struggles with loss and adversity. He lost his mother when he was a small boy. His father remarried and had a second family, which Clair didn't quite fit into. He often spent his days roaming the hillsides above Grafton or alone reading Big Little Books or mat sports stories. In time, in the St. Augustine gym on those same hillsides and at the YMCA on Main Street, he found an expression of himself in sports and athletics. The team and teammates became his family, coaches his father-substitute, and the game of basketball his lifelong passion. Clair found in this expression of himself through sports an identity that would ultimately define and justify his life. The values of family and friends that meant so much to him had a place in sports as well as life.

More importantly, what Clair Bee was able to do in writing his Chip Hilton Sports series was to embed his cherished values within a sports setting. His message was that the common values of society and religion could be learned within the game of basketball and other sports. His hero, Chip Hilton, and Chip's friends embodied the values of family, respect, friendship, sportsmanship, loyalty, and courage to do the right thing under trying circumstances. What boy would not want to be like Chip Hilton? Yet Clair Bee was not naive. He also knew the sad consequences of not following these accepted values. His stories contrasted these more ideal traits of Chip Hilton and his friends with youth whose behavior and beliefs varied from those of the ideal. The differences were made clear in a way that is meaningful and understandable.

Clair Bee's accomplishments as a basketball coach will always remain in the record books of basketball. His name will always be honored in all of basketball's Halls of Fame. But his true legacy will remain his Chip Hilton stories. It is appropriate, therefore, that these books should be reissued to make them accessible to the present and future generations of youth. Each generation needs its heroes to look to for answers to its struggles. The Chip Hilton Sports series will provide for that need today as it has for generations of the past.

Dr. Rogers McAvoy
Professor Emeritus, West Virginia University

CHAPTER 1

The Only Starter Back

MURPH KELLY, State University's head trainer, was checking the basketball medical kit when he heard noise at the door. The veteran trainer and his student assistants had just finished taping twenty pairs of ankles, and he was tired. He glanced at the two boys who had paused in the entrance to the locker room, and, for a long moment, there wasn't a sound as the gruff little man studied the athletes.

The taller athlete, Chip Hilton, stood a good four inches over six feet, and his muscular neck and sloping shoulders displayed power. But it wasn't Chip's size that attracted attention. It was the shock of blond hair, cropped in crew-cut style, and the steady gray eyes that held Murph's attention. For a brief moment Kelly's determined expression softened. Then he shifted his attention to the shorter athlete. Murph frowned impatiently. With his head of bright red hair, Soapy Smith's mischievous blue eyes and challenging expression always exasperated the hard-working trainer.

"No!" Kelly said shortly, compressing his lips and shaking his head firmly. "Absolutely, no!"

"But our grades are good, Murph," Soapy pleaded. "Chip's on the dean's list, and I'm in the top quarter of my very talented brain pool class."

"Please don't get him started, Murph." Chip grinned. "He's always talking about how his psychology classes are more difficult than everyone else's courses."

Soapy eyed Chip indignantly. "That's what I was going to say."

"That may be what you were going to say," Kelly said icily, meeting the redhead's eyes. "Regardless, I said my piece yesterday afternoon right after the football game. *No* football player is going out for basketball until he's had a week's rest! That goes for you and Hilton and Speed Morris and anybody else."

"We're not overworked, Murph," Chip assured him quickly.

"Right!" Soapy added. "And the weather's just right for basketball. Cold and snappy and—" Soapy Smith paused and glanced at Chip. "And," he gloated, "invigorating! Besides, we feel great!"

"Well, *I* don't feel great," Kelly growled.

Soapy began to count on his fingers. "OK, Murph. You're the boss," he said and smiled in resignation. "This is Friday, November the twenty-fifth. That makes one—" he paused and bristled—"one day since A & M beat us with a fluke play. No one's ever heard about a one-point safety!"

"It wasn't a fluke," Kelly interrupted. "It's right in the rule book."

"But the A & M linebacker kicked the ball out of bounds. We would have had a touchdown if he had played fair, if he had played real football."

"That's been hashed over a thousand times," Kelly said tersely. "He played according to the rules. We fumbled and the ball rolled over the A & M goal line, and the linebacker kicked the ball out of bounds for a one-point safety. It was fast thinking and smart.

"A touchdown would have meant six points. A safety usually counts for two points. In this kind of a situation, it's a one-point safety. Furthermore, we were about to fall on the ball for a touchdown that would have cost A & M the game. So A & M ends up on the long end of the score. No, Soapy, they beat us fair and square."

"Soccer players!" Soapy growled. "Well, anyway," he continued, counting on his fingers again, "today is one, and six more brings it up to Thursday, the first of December. Right?"

Kelly nodded. "Right."

"Sure!" Chip said. "But we'll miss two games: Wilson University tomorrow night and Cathedral next Wednesday."

"I don't make the schedule," Kelly said briefly. "Now why don't you would-be basketball players run along and let me get out on the court where I belong?"

"*Would-be!*" Soapy exploded. "Chip was selected to the all-American team last year and was a top scorer in the country and I, er, I—"

"Go on," Kelly urged, grinning widely. "You what?"

"Well," Soapy said lamely, "I guess *I* didn't do so well."

Kelly grunted, picked up his kit, and walked to the door leading to the gym. He grasped the knob and turned toward the two lifelong friends. "You can say that again, Smith," he said swiftly. "If I remember correctly, you didn't even make the squad!"

Soapy blinked and his mouth drooped. But only for a second. Then his jaw firmed and his blue eyes steadied. "You're right!" he agreed assertively. "But that was last year. And that's history—I'm in psychology, Murph."

"How about watching practice?" Chip asked the trainer. "All right?"

"It's all right with me," Kelly said shortly. He gestured toward the gym. "Coach Rockwell and Speed Morris are sitting up against the wall in the bleachers. If Biggie Cohen and Red Schwartz were up there, you Valley Falls High

School kids could have a reunion!" He winked and then shut the door behind him.

Soapy grimaced. "A man of principles," he said ruefully.

"More than that, Soapy. He's a tradition."

"I guess you could call him one of State's traditions," Soapy said seriously. "Just like your dad."

Chip led the way through the door and up the players' ramp to Assembly Hall's basketball court. Soapy's reference to his father had set off a chain of somber thoughts. His father *was* a tradition at State University. Big Chip Hilton had broken just about all the records in the book, in all sports. . . .

He sure gave me a great start, Chip mused, thinking about the hours his father had spent with him practicing football, basketball, and baseball in their backyard. It really wasn't too many years ago that his dad had died in a tragic industrial accident while saving a fellow employee's life.

It seemed longer, and he guessed it was because he and his mom, Mary Hilton, had worked so hard to keep their home going in Valley Falls. His mom had battled cancer the year before too. She had recovered well, but it had been a tough fight. Chip had never prayed so hard for anything in his life until then. Losing his dad had been terribly hard, but his mom had kept them together and helped him to get through it. He loved her dearly and thanked God daily for her recovery.

A slight smile crossed his lips as he remembered how she reacted the day he suggested dropping out of college and going to work full-time.

"Drop out of school?" she had repeated. "Absolutely not. Your father wanted you to graduate from State, and that's what you're going to do!"

Well, Chip thought gratefully, it hadn't been easy, but they had made it. So far at least. He had remained at State and also managed to make every football, basketball, and baseball team so far.

His heart swelled with pride as he thought of his mother's determination and courage. Her position in the telephone company in Valley Falls was something like his job at Grayson's. Both called for long hours. Someday he wanted to make it up to her.

With Soapy beside him, Chip paused on the side of the court to watch the practice. Coach Jim Corrigan was running the squad through a warm-up drill, and Chip's heart leaped. In another week, he, Soapy, and Speed would be out there with the team.

Soapy interrupted his thoughts. "Everyone around here seems to forget you're a top scorer in the country and that every game you miss makes it that much tougher for you to stay on top."

"I wasn't thinking about points, Soapy."

"Well, I was!" Soapy said gruffly. He looked around the big arena and then hooked a thumb over his shoulder. "There's the Rock and Speed," he said. "Let's join them."

Chip turned reluctantly from the floor and took the steps two at a time. Soapy followed, groaning and protesting at the pace. When they reached the top, Henry Rockwell gestured to the seat next to him, and Chip sat down by his old high school coach. Soapy moved over beside Speed Morris.

"How do they look, Coach?" Chip asked.

Rockwell smiled. "They'll look a lot better when you report," he said quietly.

"*No* height!" Speed Morris said succinctly. "It's awful tough to win without a big man in our conference."

"A big man doesn't always mean a winner," Chip protested.

"Maybe not always," Speed agreed. "But it sure helps!"

"Right!" Soapy said quickly. "You've got to control the boards. Both of them."

"One big man can't always do that," Speed objected. "Most good teams have two or three big players."

"That's what I'm talking about," Soapy said stubbornly. "Name me one championship team that didn't have a good big man!" He paused, then added, "Or a couple of them."

The redhead waited for someone to challenge his statement, but neither Chip, Speed, nor Coach Rockwell cared to debate the point. They were concentrating on the action down on the court.

Chip was thinking about the height question. Speed and Soapy were right about the importance of big men in basketball. He studied the players on the court. Rudy Slater and Dom Di Santis were the tallest men on the State squad, but they were only six-five. That didn't make them big men by a long shot.

"If only Sky Bollinger and Bill 'Burger' King were back," Soapy said thoughtfully. "They would have made the difference."

"Two six-nine men would make a lot of difference," Speed agreed sadly.

"I had hoped Bill would stay for his senior year and graduate from State. But he was in a hurry to see if he could play in the NBA. The extra year would've helped his chances, and he would have earned his degree," Rockwell observed.

"Right!" Soapy agreed. "But Bollinger could have done some studying. He's no dummy." The redhead considered the matter for a moment, then added belligerently, "Man! Sky lives at home and doesn't have to work or anything. He has plenty of time to study! He could've taken classes in the summer too. He let all of us down."

Chip agreed with Soapy but didn't say anything. Getting into college was just the beginning of it. Every player was responsible for keeping up his grades. Athletes or not, everyone had to keep working with the books.

Chip concentrated on figuring out a possible lineup. In addition to Slater and Di Santis, the returning lettermen included Jimmy Chung, Brody "Bitsy" Reardon, J. C. Tucker, Speed, and . . . wow! That was it, including himself and possibly Soapy. Soapy had been practicing every minute of his spare time for months.

Chip studied the newcomers, the sophomores. The previous year's freshman team hadn't been very successful, and Chip hadn't heard a word about any of them being outstanding. He searched them out. Only one had any size, and Chip figured him to be only about six-seven. He watched the tall, thin player move through the drill. Once was enough. The big player was too reticent and awkward—a year away, maybe two years away.

Jimmy Chung caught his eye. The little dribbling wizard had joined the team at Christmas time the previous year and had come off the bench to spark State to the Holiday Invitational Championship.

Jimmy would play, small as he was. But gone from last year's starting five were Bollinger, King, Kirk Barkley, and Andy Thornhill. Chip would be the only starter returning this year.

Chip shook his head ruefully. Speed and Soapy were right. A team—a championship team, anyway—had to have at least one big man. With a good, tall rebounder, Coach Corrigan might have started his two-year sabbatical leave with another Holiday Invitational Championship to celebrate.

Soapy had put his finger on the weak spot. Sky Bollinger *would* have made the difference. But Sky had foolishly put everything he had into basketball and neglected his studies. There was the possibility that he could recover his academic standing, but that was completely up to Sky.

"Corrigan's a good coach," Soapy said abruptly. "But he'll never win the tournament in Madison Square Garden without a big man."

Chip grinned to himself. He and Soapy had been friends for so long that their thoughts seemed to run along the same channel.

"Corrigan must want a Ph.D. pretty bad," Speed commented. "Leaving right in the middle of the season and all."

"Who's gonna take his place?" Soapy demanded. He leaned over and peered at Rockwell. "You know, Coach?"

Henry Rockwell shook his head. "No, I don't, Soapy. But I know we're going to miss Jim."

Chip nodded in affirmation and glanced sideways at his former high school coach. Valley Falls had missed Rock too. But it had been State's gain. Coach Henry Rockwell had made history at Valley Falls High School before he reached retirement age. Then, even before the news of his retirement reached the papers, he was snapped up by State's athletic department.

The Rock had always put school ahead of athletics. Woe to the player who lagged in his studies! Rock would drop him like a hot potato. Chip could still hear him. "If you can't pass your classes, you can't play! No ifs, ands, or buts!"

How many times at the end of a hard workout had he heard Rock say, "All right—not bad! Now you light out for home and hit the books. All of you! And don't be surprised if I drop by your house tonight to see what you're doing."

It was tough to get into college and tough to stay in once an athlete got there. Chip knew that he, Soapy, Speed, Biggie Cohen, and Red Schwartz owed a lot to Rock. When they were in high school, they had dreamed of being together at State. And it had all come true—largely because Rock was on their backs all the time, *on* the field and *off* the field.

A movement by Soapy caught his eye. The redhead tapped his watch.

"I know, Soapy," he said. "Let's go."

"We're off!" Soapy said briskly. "I'm sure you will excuse Mr. Hilton and myself, er, Coach, Mr. Morris. You see, ahem, we have an important board meeting at Grayson's."

"Sure!" Speed said quickly. "We'll excuse you. In fact, I think I'll go along with you. I want to see what kind of board meeting a hardheaded burger-flipper and a stockroom clerk can hold."

"I think you're figuring on a burger and an extra scoop of ice cream," Soapy said quickly. "Well, let me set you straight, Mr. Morris. You get what you pay for at *our* place."

"How much do you pay Grayson to let you work behind the fountain?" Speed gibed. "You must have put on twenty pounds since yesterday."

"Whaddaya mean?" Soapy gasped, sucking in his stomach and squaring his shoulders. "Look! I'm in perfect shape. Tell him, Coach."

"Oh, sure!" Speed interrupted. "Murph Kelly thinks you look the best in a basketball uniform."

Soapy snorted. "Hah! Murph Kelly wouldn't give me a second glance if I was seven feet tall."

Rockwell laughed. "If you were seven feet tall, Soapy," he said, "Murph Kelly would follow you around day and night. Right now, Corrigan and Kelly would give their right arms for a big, talented pivot man."

CHAPTER 2

A Big Man's Game

CHIP HILTON led the way out of Assembly Hall and took the shortcut across campus to University's business district. His long strides carried him rapidly along, but Soapy and Speed didn't like it. The two wranglers joined forces against him and blocked his path.

"Take it easy, Chip," Soapy pleaded.

"Yeah," Speed added, "where's the fire?"

"At Grayson's," Chip said, grinning. "Less than thirty shopping days to Christmas. Remember?"

"And only twenty-seven more days until the big tournament in New York," Soapy quipped. "Broadway, here we come! Turn on all those bright lights!" Spinning around on his toes, his arms outstretched, Soapy exclaimed, "I *love* New York!"

"You can forget the city and those Broadway lights if we don't win a couple of games," Speed grumbled. "We'll no sooner get there then we'll have to turn around and come home."

"The lights in Madison Square Garden are all I want to see," Chip said wistfully.

Soapy snorted. "The fans will want to see you! Wonder what the Garden scoring record is."

"Seventy-one points," Speed said.

"Chip will break it," Soapy said confidently. "He broke the record at Springfield, didn't he?"

"Madison Square Garden is a long way from Springfield," Chip said.

"That might be true," Soapy agreed, "but the teams aren't any better."

Speed nodded. "Right! We played most of them last year: Southwestern, Eastern, Mercer, Wesleyan, Dane University, and Wilson University."

"Southwestern is the powerhouse," Soapy asserted.

"Means nothing," Speed said quickly. "We beat them in the Springfield Invitational after they had won forty-nine straight."

"*And*," Soapy added significantly, "Southwestern won the NCAA Championship."

"That's right," agreed Chip, "but last year we had Bollinger and King. We could match their big men then."

"We're not going to match up against any big men this year," Speed said bitterly. "If you ask me, there are too many big men playing basketball. Someone ought to do something about it."

"You saw what Bill Bell said in the *Herald,* didn't you?" Soapy asked. Without waiting for a reply, the redhead plunged in. "Bell said the rules ought to be changed so there would be height divisions in basketball like the weight divisions in boxing and wrestling."

"I don't think we'll get very far with this debate, guys," Chip remarked sadly. "Anyway, it isn't going to help us this year."

"There are more big guys dominating basketball now than ever before," Speed said. "It's a big man's game."

"Not quite," Chip said. "We're not exactly big, and we're doing all right."

"You've got that right!" Soapy agreed. "Look what Jimmy Chung did to Southwestern last year in the Springfield Invitational! And how about Bitsy Reardon? He grew over the summer, but he's still only five-eight or five-nine."

"Sure!" Speed agreed. "We beat them, but we didn't win the title. And now that we're on the subject—who did win it?"

"Southwestern!" Soapy said.

"And they had five big men," Speed said significantly. "With three of them on the starting five."

"You couldn't call their backcourt men small either," Chip said dryly.

"Man, you can say that again," Speed agreed. "They didn't have anyone on the squad who was less than six-three, and they're supposed to be even bigger this year."

"They're like football players on the basketball court," Soapy growled. "Elbows, knees, pushing, shoving, holding—"

"They came by that naturally enough," Speed said bitterly. "That's the only kind of basketball Jeff Habley and Rip Ritter teach."

"That's why we're lucky to have a coach like Jim Corrigan," Chip said.

The three friends had reached the main shopping district now, and their conversation slowed as they threaded their way through the crowded streets. When they reached the corner of State and Tenth, they paused in front of one of Grayson's big windows.

What had begun as a small family pharmacy in University nearly thirty years earlier had mushroomed into a major retail establishment selling everything from toiletries to beach towels to greeting cards to gift items. George Grayson, ever mindful of the college students, had purchased the two adjoining buildings and expanded his business to include an old-fashioned soda fountain, a modern food court, and a "sports center," including video games, several comfortable couches, and a big-screen TV.

Grayson's was a huge success and attracted both the town's local residents and the college students, who packed the fountain and food court every afternoon and evening.

Inside, behind the crowded fountain, Chip could see Fred "Fireball" Finley and Philip "Whitty" Whittemore. The two football stars were moving briskly from customer to customer.

"Let's go, Soapy," he said anxiously. "Fireball and Whitty are snowed under."

"I'll skip the board meeting this time, Soapy," Speed laughed. "This place is jammed. See you later."

"How about meeting us after work?" Chip asked.

"Pete's?"

"Where else?" Soapy demanded. "A working man has to eat."

Speed groaned. "All the time? Wait!" he added quickly. "Don't answer that! I'll be there."

Mitzi Savrill was making change for a customer, but she paused in the middle of her count to flash a quick smile toward her two coworkers. Chip nodded to her and hurried on toward the stockroom in the back of the store, but Soapy slowed down.

The violet-blue-eyed cashier was Soapy's "true love," and he never passed up an opportunity to bask in her lovely presence. Chip grinned as he caught the view from over his shoulder. The redhead stopped and leaned on the change counter, waiting for Mitzi to finish her counting.

Chip continued on and glanced at the clock over the stockroom door. It was five minutes to four and his assistant, Skip Miller, was due any minute. He opened the door and paused. Skip was already there. The high school star athlete was standing in front of the desk with his back to the door, checking some order sheets.

Chip studied his assistant. He always got a strange feeling when he looked at Skip because the two of them looked enough alike to be brothers. Skip was six-two, weighed 185 pounds, and had the same type of build as Chip.

Like himself, Skip had gray eyes and blond hair. Except for the four-year difference in their ages and a few inches in height, they might have passed as twins. He would have liked that, Chip reflected. Skip was more than a great high school athlete; he was a good person. He was friendly, likable, a hard worker, and ambitious.

Skip turned and started in surprise. "Chip! You startled me. How long have you been standing there?"

"I just got here. You're early."

"Sure! Good reason too! Mr. Grayson was talking to me yesterday, and he said I would be in charge while you were away for the tournament."

Skip paused for a second and then continued excitedly, "You know what? He said he was going to give me a raise. How about that?"

"Great!"

"I gather Murph Kelly wouldn't let you practice."

"No, he wouldn't. But you know Soapy. Every no is a challenge."

"Did you watch the workout?"

"We stayed for a little while with Speed and Coach Rockwell," Chip answered.

"How do they look?"

"Fine. Just one drawback—no height."

"No big men at all?" Skip questioned.

Chip shook his head and frowned. "No one you could really call big."

"How about Rudy Slater?"

"He's six-five, Skip. He's a good forward, but he hasn't had much experience playing around the pivot area."

"Coach Corrigan seem worried?"

Chip nodded ruefully. "He's not the only one."

"Corrigan will come up with something," Skip said confidently.

"I guess we'd better come up with some of those orders you're looking at," Chip said, smiling. "Let's get with it."

Skip left at nine o'clock, and an hour later Chip sat down at the desk. It was his first break since six, when Soapy had brought him a sandwich from the fountain. Idly he began to scribble a lineup on a piece of paper. When Chip finished, he studied the heights written beside each name and shook his head ruefully.

Jimmy Chung	5'10"
Speed Morris	5'11"-6'
Bitsy Reardon	5'8"-5'9"
Rudy Slater	6'5"
C. H.	6'4"

"It's the best lineup," he muttered, "but it barely averages six feet. We've got to have a big man!"

The sound of hurrying feet stopped his thoughts. Soapy barged through the door, followed by his fellow fountaineers, Whitty and Fireball. "I'm bushed," Soapy said wearily. He dropped down on a chair next to the desk and pulled off his shoes. "Don't the students in this town ever eat at the student union?"

"Be glad they don't," Whitty laughed. "Without them, we'd be out of jobs."

"Never mind them," Fireball Finley said. "Let's go get *us* something to eat. I'm starved."

"Just a second and I'll be ready," Chip said. He cleared the desk, cast a quick look around the stockroom, and followed his three friends through the darkened store. Soapy led the way out the side door and along Tenth Street to Pete Thorpe's restaurant.

There were only two or three customers sitting at the long counter, and the booths along the opposite side of the room were empty.

Jimmy Chung smiled broadly and waved them to their usual booth. "Your private table, gentlemen," he said, bowing in mock deference.

Then the little basketball star turned toward the kitchen. "Pete!" he called. "Chip Hilton and those football players from Grayson's are here."

"Throw 'em out!" the restaurant owner bellowed. A moment later he came out of the kitchen. Wiping his hands on his apron, he playfully strode over to the booth.

"You see, Jimmy," he said, nodding at his counterman, "it's just like I told you. Grayson's is a real fancy place all right. But the man who knows good food ends up right here at little ole Pete's Place."

"Right!" Soapy said. "Now, me—I want a thick, juicy steak with some crinkle-cut french fries and a salad with pepper-corn dressing and whole wheat bread—" He paused and looked around the booth at his smiling friends. "I've got to watch my weight, you know."

"We know," Fireball chortled.

"Don't you college kids ever eat at the student union?" Pete asked.

The whole booth erupted into laughter, and Pete gave them a surprised look.

The phone rang, and Jimmy hurried over to the counter to answer it. He listened for a second and turned toward the booth.

"Chip!" he called. "It's for you."

"Wonder who that could be?" Chip said, getting wearily to his feet.

Finley glanced warily at Soapy. "It's Mitzi," he goaded.

"She's really looking for me," Soapy said brightly.

"You mean she doesn't even know your name?" Whitty asked with mock incredulity.

"She knows my name," Soapy said smugly. "She just doesn't want everyone to know how she feels about me."

Whitty and Fireball caught each other's glances and cried in unison, "Not!"

Chip laughed as he picked up the phone. It was Skip Miller, and his voice reflected his excitement. "Chip," he said breathlessly, "good news! I've got a big man for you!"

"You're kidding!"

"No, I'm not."

"Is he in school? Is he a State student?"

"He sure is! He's a junior."

Chip shook his head. "He can't be very big," he said tentatively.

"He not only *can* be, but *is!*"

"How tall?"

Skip laughed exultantly. "So tall that he has to duck to get through a door."

"Does he play basketball?"

"I don't know how good he is, but he plays. Herb Harris, one of my teammates, saw him at the Y. Herb says he works there after school, in the afternoons. Herb thinks he's about seven feet tall."

"Seven feet! Can't be. How come he isn't out for the team?"

"I don't know anything about that, Chip. Herb came over to my house to study tonight, and we got to talking about you and big men and State, and, well, that's all I know."

It was too good to be true. There had to be a catch to it. "What's his name, Skip? Where does he live?"

"I don't know, Chip. Herb doesn't either. But I can go over to the Y tomorrow afternoon and find out. I just thought you would like to hear the good news tonight."

"You're sure right, Skip. Thanks a million. And Skip, don't worry about tomorrow afternoon. I'll be at the Y myself."

Skip chuckled. "I thought you would," he said. "See ya later."

Chip could scarcely restrain his exuberance. If Skip had uncovered a big man who could play any kind of ball at all, State's worries were over. His friends quickly noticed Chip's excitement and looked at him expectantly as he returned to the booth.

"What's up?" Soapy asked.

"Corrigan's offense," Chip said, grinning. "His defense too!"

The redhead's blue eyes brightened sharply. "Corrigan's offense and defense?"

"That's right. If the news I just got from Skip Miller is right."

"What news?" Jimmy Chung asked.

"Let me guess!" Soapy interrupted eagerly. "Skip knows a big man. Right?"

"So Skip knows a big man," Speed said. "How can that help? There're lots of big men in this world. Corrigan needs a big man *now*. Quicker than now! In school and eligible!"

Soapy studied Chip for a brief second. "He is in school!" he said confidently. "Right, Chip?"

Chip nodded and looked around the circle of faces. Whitty and Fireball were waiting patiently for his reply. There was an expression of doubtful yet hopeful curiosity on Speed's face.

Pete and Jimmy had forgotten all about their customers. The whole group was watching Chip intently, hanging on his words. But it was Soapy who held Chip's attention. The accuracy of the redhead's intuitive thinking was amazing.

"That's right, Soapy," he said. "Skip says there's a junior in school who is seven feet tall."

Soapy leaped to his feet. "Seven!" he echoed. "You mean he's actually seven feet tall?"

"That's what Skip said."

"But can he play basketball?" Speed asked.

"That," Chip said firmly, "I mean to find out! Tomorrow!"

CHAPTER 3

Great with Kids

THE YMCA BUILDING was just ahead, and Chip breathed a sigh of relief. He glanced back at the crowded shopping section of Main Street and farther back to Grayson's on the corner of Main and State. He had walked the few short blocks between the store and the Y many, many times during the past year. Usually he would window-shop as he walked leisurely along. That thought carried him back to the previous basketball season when he had been laid up a short time with a knee injury. While his leg had been on the mend, he had limbered it up almost every day at the Y.

He tried to slow his purposeful and urgent pace. There was really no great hurry, he reflected. He had plenty of time. In fact, he had not been rushed all morning. There was never much of a rush in the stockroom on Saturday mornings. He tried once more to slow down, but it was no use, so he resumed his fast pace. In a few minutes he reached the Y building and took the steps leading to the main entrance three at a time. He found John Ward, the secretary, behind the lobby desk, right inside the door.

Ward looked up with a warm smile and then glanced at the clock. "Hiya, Chip," he said in a surprised voice. "What are you doing here? You ought to be resting up for tonight's game."

"I guess you don't know Murph Kelly very well," Chip laughed. "I'm not playing." Then he explained that the State University trainer had decided he and the rest of the football players needed a rest following the long football season. While he talked, Chip focused on the purpose of his visit. He could hardly wait to voice his thoughts.

"Say, Mr. Ward," he said, "is it true that one of the guys who works here is around seven feet tall? Or, as Soapy would say, excuse the pun, 'Is that just a tall story?'"

Ward smiled and eyed Chip inquisitively. "Don't tell me you haven't met Branch Phillips?"

Chip shook his head. "No, I haven't. Is he around?"

"He should be here any minute. Branch works in our youth division on Saturday afternoons. He works during the week after school too. He's great with kids."

"Skip Miller says he goes to State," Chip ventured.

"That's true, Chip. I'm surprised the two of you haven't met. He's a junior. I think he's an agriculture or forestry major."

So that's it, Chip was thinking. That's the reason he hadn't run into Phillips around the campus. The agricultural campus, with the forestry school, was five miles out in the country. Aloud, he said, "Now I understand why I haven't seen him."

"That isn't the only reason you haven't seen him," Ward said. "Branch lights out for home when he gets through with work. His family lives on a large farm in the timber section north of here. It's one of the few remaining family farms around here. I think it's about ten miles out."

"Does he play basketball?" Chip asked, trying to speak casually.

Ward deliberated a moment. "Actually, Chip," he said, "I never saw him play. But I've watched him shoot around in the gym with the kids. The youngsters think he's the greatest; they brag about him all the time."

John paused and nodded understandingly. "I know what you're thinking. I've been reading the papers. I guess everyone in town knows about Corrigan's big-man problem."

"*Big* is right," Chip said dryly. "I wonder why Branch never came out for basketball?"

"I don't really know, Chip, but I have a hunch it's because he has to work. His father is dead, I understand, and he's more or less the head of the family."

"How long has he been working here?"

"This is his second year. I do know that this job is pretty important to him."

"Do you think he might give basketball a try? That is, if the coaches say it's OK?"

Ward glanced over Chip's shoulder. "Why don't you ask him yourself?" he said lightly. "Here he comes!"

Chip moved to one side and turned to watch Branch Phillips walk briskly up to the desk and sign in. Chip had expected to see a tall, skinny, and gangly sort of person. He was certainly surprised.

Branch Phillips was rawboned, but he was well proportioned and built like an athlete. He had alert brown eyes and a prominent nose. His fair complexion seemed at odds with his dark brown hair. Chip judged him to weigh in the neighborhood of 230 pounds. He walked with a slight stoop and carried his head bent forward on his long neck. There was no question that he was close to seven feet in height.

"Hello, Branch," Ward said. He gestured toward Chip. "I want you to meet Chip Hilton. I guess you've heard *that* name before."

"Chip *Hilton!*"

"That's right. Chip, this is Branch Phillips."

Phillips stared at Chip for a brief moment and then his hand shot swiftly out. "I'll say I've heard that name. Man, I guess just about everybody has."

Chip smiled and shook hands with Branch. His own fingers were long and he had a powerful grip, but his hand was lost in Branch's big one. Chip was surprised, too, to find that Branch's big hand was as hard as a rock, and he had a grip like a vise.

"Wow!" Chip said when Phillips released his hand. "What a grip!"

"Sorry 'bout that. I do a lot of work with my hands," Phillips explained. "Besides, they're pretty big."

"I'll say they are!"

"Chip's been waiting to meet you, Branch," John Ward interrupted.

Phillips's eyes widened in surprise. "Me?"

"That's right. Why don't you take him in the gym and get him to shoot a few baskets? He holds the national scoring record, you know."

"I know," Phillips said quickly. "Forty-three points a game! Every one of the kids in the youth division knows Chip's record. I'm sure they'd like to meet him."

"Well," John Ward said, "here's your chance. The kids will be here in a few minutes. Get Chip a pair of shoes and sweats." He turned to Chip. "All right with you?"

Chip nodded. "Sure, Mr. Ward. I'm not due at Grayson's for at least an hour."

As Mr. Ward unlocked the equipment room and dug out a ball, Branch showed Chip to the locker room and tossed him some sweats and a pair of shoes. As Chip tried on the shoes, he used the time to get to know Branch.

"Mr. Ward tells me you're a junior in the ag school," Chip said.

"That's right. I grew up on a working farm, so I'm about halfway finished on a forestry degree and taking some ag courses too. What else would someone with my name do?" Branch laughed.

"How come you never came out for basketball at State? For the freshman team or as a walk-on for the varsity?"

"Uh . . . I'm no good at basketball, Chip. I'm too clumsy. At least that's what one of the coaches at Southwestern told me."

"You mean Southwestern University?"

Branch nodded. "That's right. I went to school there for a year."

"What happened?"

"It's a long story."

"I have plenty of time."

"Well, I went to a little high school out in the country near here and I played basketball my last year." He paused and shrugged his shoulders. "I guess the coach let me play because I was so tall.

"Anyway, when I graduated, Mr. Ritter from Southwestern came to the house and talked to me about going to school at Southwestern. He said it wouldn't cost our family anything. He said something about grants and scholarship money. It sounded wonderful at the time. Anyway, my mother said I could go."

He hesitated a moment. "My father died, Chip, and I had been taking care of the farm. Well, I went there in September, and when the basketball season started, I reported for the team workouts."

"Who was the coach?"

"It was the same man who came to see me when I got out of high school, Mr. Ritter."

"Rip Ritter?"

Phillips nodded.

"How did things go?"

Phillips smiled ruefully. "Not very well. They had a lot of big guys who were a lot better than me."

"I know," Chip said grimly. His thoughts shot back to State's two games against Southwestern the previous season. Phillips was right. There had been half a dozen players on the Southwestern team who were six-six or better.

"Anyway," Phillips continued, "Coach Ritter worked with me for a couple of weeks and then one day he got mad and said I would never be a basketball player."

"What happened then?"

"Well, Mr. Ritter said he guessed he had been wrong about me and that he would have to give the scholarship to someone else."

"Did you finish out the year?"

"Yes," Phillips said bitterly, "I finished out the year, but my mother had to borrow money for books and tuition. I worked and that covered my room and meals. Mom also had to hire someone to take care of the tree work for the farm and to cover the firewood route. It was too much for her. When the school year was over, I came back home and Mom and I talked about it. I figured I'd better forget basketball and apply to State and take up forestry or farming. So that's what I did."

"Hasn't anyone ever talked to you about playing basketball here at State?"

"Oh, sure. Coach Corrigan and Coach Sullivan and a few friends and other people. It's pretty tough to hide when you're this tall," Branch grinned.

"What did you say to Coach Corrigan?"

"I told him about Southwestern and how things were at home . . . ." Phillips paused and shrugged.

"What did he say?"

"He said I could have the same kind of grant or scholarship I had been promised at Southwestern."

"Why didn't you take it?"

"Well, there was the money Mom had to borrow and the way she felt about basketball. My time at the Y is a break from work and studies, plus it's a little extra money. But taking care of the trees—the pruning and thinning—takes a lot of time. We also have a seasonal firewood route and a Christmas tree business." He shook his head grimly. "Then there was the way I was treated at Southwestern. That was hard to take. I never thought college coaches were like that. He promised a scholarship and then practically threw me out of school in the middle of the year."

"State's coaches aren't like that," Chip said. "In fact, I don't believe there are more than two or three coaches in the whole country who operate that way. You just ran into the wrong one."

"I sure did! Anyway, I'm too awkward to play basketball."

"Coach Corrigan could take care of the awkward part of it."

"Maybe," Branch said doubtfully. He shook his head and then continued quickly, "Don't think I wouldn't love to play. That's one of my greatest ambitions. Everyone seems to think I can play basketball just because I'm tall, I guess."

"What makes you think you can't?"

"Well, Mr. Ritter is a coach, and I guess he ought to know. I was pretty upset when I came home and I made up my mind to show Mr. Ritter I *could* be a basketball player. That's partly why I got the job here at the Y.

"I've practiced pretty hard on shooting and dribbling and jumping, but I've never had time to play against someone my own age, so I don't know whether I'm any good or not. I do know I can shoot—" Phillips smiled in embarrassment. "Well, I can shoot a little better."

"Let's find out how good you are," Chip said quickly. "You change clothes, and I'll shoot around."

While Branch was in the locker room, Chip took the ball and walked out on the small court used by the youth program. He warmed up with a few layups from the left and right sides, then took some free throws from the foul line. By the time Branch joined him on the court, Chip had loosened up and was hitting shots regularly from behind the three-point line.

As soon as Branch stepped out on the court, Chip flipped the ball to him. Phillips was taken by surprise. He reached clumsily for the ball, but it bounded out of his hands and dropped to the floor. Phillips was embarrassed. "See, I told you," he said. "I can't even catch the ball."

"You weren't ready," Chip said, stooping to pick up the ball. "Let your hands give a little."

Phillips extended his hands and looked down at them. "They're pretty stiff," he said.

"That's no real handicap," Chip said. "You've got tremendous hands, and that's a big asset in basketball. Let's try it again. This time reach out for the ball and then pull your hands back just as the ball reaches them. That makes a sort of cushion. Get it?"

Chip soon forgot all about Grayson's. Branch appeared awkward, but his great height made up for it. Chip worked with the eager student on passing and shooting for half an hour. And with every passing minute, his exultation rose. Phillips *could* be the answer. The big college junior could shoot and he'd even followed with slam dunks on a couple of shots. He could get up high enough on the boards to aid State.

On one shot, Chip noticed that Branch's elbows had been above the basket when he grabbed the ball off the boards. *All Branch Phillips needs to be a good basketball player,* Chip was thinking, *is a coach like Corrigan—a coach who is understanding and has a lot of patience.*

Chip was on the verge of asking Phillips about coming out for varsity basketball as a walk-on when several youngsters slipped quietly into the gym and stood along the wall. They were watching with eager eyes, anxious to get onto the court. The opportunity was lost. It was time to call it a day and let the kids have the gym.

"Branch, I need to get to work, but I'd like to meet with you again sometime. Would that be OK?"

"Sure! This was great. I'm here at the Y at four each afternoon. Drop by sometime."

When Chip reached Grayson's, Soapy was busy behind the fountain making ice cream sundaes. But the redhead's questioning eyes followed him all the way back to the stock-room. And with the first lull, Soapy rushed back to learn the news. "Is he really seven feet tall? Is he any good? Can he run the floor? Shoot? Pass? Slam dunk? Rebound? Is he coming out for the team?"

Chip nodded and smiled. One never had a chance to answer Soapy when he started one of his tirades. Soapy had to go on until he ran out of breath.

"Yes, he's seven feet tall, Soapy. And he's got a lot of possibilities. He can shoot and he's fast. He doesn't have a lot of confidence in what he can do, but that's understandable. I didn't have a chance to ask him about coming out for the team."

"Whaddaya mean you didn't have a chance to ask him? What were you doing all that time?"

"He had to work, Soapy. I couldn't take up any more of his time."

"Take up more of his time? Come on, Chip!" The disappointed expression on Soapy's face remained for a moment and then transformed into a wide smile. "I've got it! How about *tonight?* You're going to the game, aren't you? You've got to go! Mr. Grayson said you ought to go too! Besides, you owe it to the team. Right?"

Chip nodded. "Yes, that's right, Soapy."

"So!" Soapy said, cocking his head to one side. "Why don't you ask this Branch Phillips guy to go with you?"

Chip eyed Soapy and grinned. "Soapy," he said happily, "you're a genius! That's exactly what I'm going to do. Tell Skip I'll be right back."

CHAPTER 4

A Tall Order

ANXIOUS TO SEE State's opening game of the season, students and fans were pouring into State University's famous Assembly Hall when Chip and Branch approached the broad steps leading to the main entrance of the building.

A light snow was falling, and most of the fans were walking carefully, fearful of slipping and falling. But Branch Phillips's height drew their attention, and when they recognized Chip Hilton, they gave way and opened a path for them to pass through. Some of the students were Chip's classmates, and they slapped him on the back and greeted him with friendly comments. Other people who had never seen him except on the football field or basketball court elbowed their companions and pointed him out. Branch's height drew gasps of surprise from all of them.

"Hey there, Chip! How ya doin', bud?"

"Hurry up, Hilton! You're late!"

"He isn't playing! Don't you read the papers?"

"Who's that big guy? I know the shorter one, that guy is Hilton, but who's—"

"So that's Hilton. I thought he was taller."

"He's tall enough. Six-four!"

"Then that other guy must be seven feet tall. Wonder who he is?"

"I don't know who he is, but I know State could use him."

"You got that right! I read in the paper that Corrigan's tallest returning man is only six-five."

"The big guy must be a freshman."

The freshman game ended just as Chip and Branch reached the row of seats behind the State bench. And once again Chip and Branch drew the attention of the fans. Andre Gilbert, one of State's basketball managers, had been standing in front of the scorers' table, scanning the crowd. As soon as he saw Chip, he spoke to the usher and walked up to the seats behind the bench.

"Man," he said, leaning over to grasp Chip's hand, "am I glad to see you! It's nearly eight o'clock."

"Why did you want to see me?"

"Coach was asking for you," Andre said nonchalantly. "Guess he wanted to be sure you got to see the game."

"We made it, weather and all. Andre, this is Branch Phillips. Branch, shake hands with a terrific manager, Andre Gilbert."

Gilbert shook hands with Phillips and eyed him appraisingly.

"Things seem to be looking up," he smiled widely.

"Maybe," Chip said, glancing at Branch.

"Wish you were playing tonight, Chip," Andre said.

The din of Assembly Hall decreased slightly, but suddenly a burst of cheers broke out near the players' aisle. It turned into a tremendous roar as the white-clad State players ran along the sideline and aligned themselves in front of the State University bench. The courtside announcer tried several times to break through the cheers before he got the attention of the fans.

"Let me have your attention, please. Just a moment now, thank you! Now hear this! One of State's basketball traditions is the election of a captain just before the first game of the season. The selection this year—"

The announcer paused for a moment, and Chip saw Coach Corrigan turn toward him and grin. Then it hit him. Now he understood why Andre had seemed so relieved to see him at the game.

"This season," the announcer continued, "the selection will undoubtedly surprise no one except State's great all-American star, the one and only—"

The announcer's words were lost in a roar that grew louder and louder, and then Andre Gilbert pulled Chip out of his seat, over the bench, and onto the court. Coach Corrigan handed Chip a ball, and Jimmy Chung, Dom, J. C., Rudy, and Bitsy all tried to shake his hand at once. With serious game-time faces, they each congratulated Chip and let him know they respected him as their team leader, a responsibility he understood and accepted. All Chip could think of during the celebration was how honored he was to play at State University with this great group of guys and for Coach Corrigan.

Then Coach Corrigan grabbed his hand and pulled him farther out on the floor so the photographers could get some pictures. The lights of the TV cameras from the local stations prevented him from looking up into the stands, and all he could hear were the State cheerleaders and the jazz band leading a cheer for their new captain.

Moments later, a reporter came hustling up with the Wilson University captain, and there were more picture taking and handshaking until he thought it would never end and the game would never be played. He finally escaped from center court, tossed the ball to Jimmy Chung with a serious nod, and scrambled back to his seat.

But that didn't end it. The State fans sitting around him gave him another warm reception until he wished he could sink right down through his seat to the floor. His heart was thumping and his ears were burning and he wanted to get away from all the noise and acclaim, but with it all, he felt a great burst of pride well up in his chest.

He thought of his mom at home in Valley Falls and hoped fervently that she had the TV in the family room tuned in to Gee-Gee Gray's program. He looked up at the press booth and he could see the red eye of the television camera trained directly at him, so he turned his head away to talk with Branch, his face burning.

Branch Phillips leaned close. "Wow, Chip," he said breathlessly. "Am I ever glad you invited me to the game tonight. I sure am proud to be with you. This is one of the greatest things that's ever happened to me."

Chip smiled and nodded. It was one of the greatest things that had ever happened to him too. It was a great honor, and even more than that, it was a great responsibility. And it would be a long time before he forgot this night. Being elected captain of a team before a player had even been out to practice was really something very special!

The State cheering squads appeared then, and Chip breathed a sigh of relief. Now the fans would have someone else to look at and talk about. While the cheerleaders were getting organized, he glanced toward the scorers' table and was surprised to see Coach Corrigan standing there. He was about to comment on the coach's presence when the visitors trotted out along the sideline and lined up in front of their bench.

"They're pretty big, Chip," Branch whispered.

Chip nodded grimly but said nothing. He remembered most of them well. He thought back to the game with Wilson University the previous year. It had been a lucky win for State. He and his teammates had pulled out a squeaker for a tough win by a single point, 89-88. And in the Holiday Invitational, Wilson had gone on to the semifinals. He studied their faces and their composure for a moment, and his heart sank. It was a veteran team.

Both teams went into their warm-up drills, and Chip again sized up the visitors. The Wilson University coach had brought a squad of twelve men, and they were all tall. Seven of them easily had their elbows above the rim as they rebounded errant warm-up shots. Chip shifted his attention to the State players and the great difference in the height of the two squads. It was startlingly obvious. There wasn't much doubt about which team would control the boards in this game.

Cheers from the fans swept through the hall, echoing from side to side as game time approached. The State University male cheerleaders ran the length of the court waving gigantic red, white, and blue banners as the cheerleading squad somersaulted the width of the court. As the banners swept from corner to corner in Assembly Hall, the crowd joined in the cheers of "GO BIG RED! GO BIG RED!" and "GO STATE!"

Players at both ends of the court were taking their last few shots from their favorite spots and working in a few free throws as the clock wound down to the sound of the buzzer when it reached 00:00. The warm-up was over. The State University basketball season was about to get underway. The five starters on each team had removed their warm-ups as Chip named State's lineup for Branch.

"Dom Di Santis at center, Rudy Slater and J. C. Tucker at forwards, Jimmy Chung and Bitsy Reardon at guards."

"It isn't a very big team," Branch said, his forehead creased in a slight frown. Chip nodded but didn't say anything. He was studying the Wilson players on the court.

The three officials walked from the scorers' table where they had been standing since the pregame activity began. They had checked with the scorers and the timekeeper, and now they shook hands with both head coaches.

A moment later Jimmy Chung walked out to the center circle where the officials waited. A tall Wilson University player also joined the group. The two opponents shook hands, listened attentively to the officials' instructions, and trotted back to the sidelines. While this was going on, Assembly Hall's home announcer was naming each team's starting five, but it was hard to hear the names because of the noise of the crowd.

Then the announcer introduced the student who would sing "The Star-Spangled Banner," and everyone stood up and proudly faced the flag. With the last chord of the song, the referee blasted his whistle, and the players walked out to their tip-off positions.

The State players lined up beside their respective opponents, and Chip groaned when he noted the size of the Wilson players. He quickly checked their numbers in the game program and read the statistics aloud. "Henninger, center: six-ten! Jones, forward: six-seven. Argento, forward: six-six. Grant, guard: six-four. Murray, guard: six-three."

The cheerleaders were trying to lead a cheer, but the noise from the crowd drowned them out. Then the ball was in the air and the game was on. The big Wilson center leaped high in the air and tapped the ball back far behind him. The Wilson guards blocked the State forwards on the play, and the visitors' forwards dashed back and controlled the ball. Chip could tell that Wilson's superior height was already being put to work.

And Chip knew what was coming. The big center trotted down to a position near his basket just outside the three-second lane. Meanwhile, his teammates were advancing the ball slowly into their front court. Right then, on the very first play, the pattern of the Wilson attack was revealed. The visitors waited until the center was set, passed quickly to the right corner, used a clear-out to free the big pivot man for a pass, and then gave him the ball.

Di Santis was trying to work to a position in front of the Wilson center, but he just couldn't make it. The big pivot man was too tall and strong and had too much savvy. He held Di Santis off with his body, stretched his arms out at full length, and gathered in the ball. Then he wheeled and banked it swiftly and surely against the board for the first basket of the game.

Reardon took the ball out of bounds and passed to Chung. Jimmy dribbled upcourt at full speed. Then he passed to Rudy Slater, cut around the outside, and broke free. Slater whipped the ball back to Jimmy and he drove for the basket. Then, just as the little speedster attempted the layup, one of the center's long arms snaked forward. His big hand took the ball practically off Jimmy Chung's fingertips.

That was the pattern of the first half.

The Statesmen managed to get a few outside shots, but they seldom got a close one and never a second shot.

The big Wilson center and forwards covered both backboards like a blanket. When a Wilson shot missed the hoop, the ball was tapped up again and again until it fell through the net. It was more like volleyball than basketball. And that was Wilson's game plan for the first half. State's opponents were just too big. The score at the half: Wilson 46, State 28.

All around Chip and Branch, the fans were talking about the size of the visitors. Most of them were making excuses for the Statesmen, but there were many who were sarcastic and bitter in their denunciation of Corrigan. Chip felt a red flame creep up his neck to his ears, but he kept quiet and listened.

"Other teams seem to have the big men. How come Corrigan can't get out and dig up a couple?"

"You're forgetting King and Bollinger."

"So what! University should have been prepared."

"You mean he should do more recruiting?"

"Of course! That's the name of the game today."

"Perhaps State needs better recruiters on the coaching staff."

"You got it! Corrigan is leaving, so what does he care?"

Chip wished he could reply to that statement. He knew what State did for athletes and how dedicated Coach Corrigan was to the university, the team, and each player.

Chip's thoughts were interrupted by a burst of cheers from the loyal State fans. The Statesmen were coming back out for the second half, and they were full of fight. They weren't giving up and he wasn't either. He glanced at Phillips. Branch had sat all through the halftime intermission, looking straight ahead or down at his program, shifting his feet nervously, and clasping and unclasping his big hands as he heard the fans talking around them.

"Don't worry, Branch," Chip said, elbowing his new friend. "Things will be different during the second half."

"I hope so, but I don't see how," Branch said dejectedly.

"Coach will use the press," Chip said confidently. "We used it last year when we lost our big men."

"Then why didn't he use it in the first half?"

"Coach Corrigan likes to hold his strategy until the second half."

The teams were back out on the court, and the fans were shouting and yelling and cheering. The referee handed the ball to Bitsy for State's throw-in to start the second half. It was a sloppy inbounds pass, and the alert Wilson defender tapped the ball away from Jimmy's outstretched hands.

Wilson was in control again. But this time the Statesmen played aggressive defense and went after opposing players, hustling them all over the court, taking chances, trying for interceptions, lunging, chasing, slapping at the ball, and trying desperately to break up the slow pattern the visitors had used so effectively in the first half.

It nearly worked, but not quite. Once again, the overpowering height of Wilson's team took its toll. The Wilson players elevated the plane of their passes. Their big men dashed down the court and away from their teammates, only to fishhook back and leap high in the air for the ball. Then the smaller men would cut by for a return pass and dribble in for a score. Wilson took the press in stride.

"They remember from last year," Chip murmured to himself. "All of the teams we played last year will be ready for it."

The Statesmen were fighting their hearts out. They never let up and never backed down. They made a good number of interceptions and converted them into baskets.

But Wilson kept pace and matched basket for basket. It was an exciting game, and the fans enjoyed the wild play, the daring dashes, and the mad scrambles for the ball. But the final score was never really in doubt. There could be only one ending to the debacle, and Chip was glad when the buzzer ended the game. The final score: Wilson University 96, State University 70.

Many of the fans departed before the game ended. They were anxious to beat the crowd out of Assembly Hall and the packed parking lot surrounding the large facility. Others lingered, took their time, and accepted the fact that they would be held up by the hundreds of cars parked outside.

Some of the fans were disgruntled and voiced their disappointment. But the great majority accepted the defeat philosophically, keenly aware that the home team had been outmanned. The crowd's chatter summed it up correctly and succinctly.

"State just doesn't have board strength."

"We didn't have Hilton."

"What could he have done against a big man like Henninger? Nothing!"

"You mean what could he have done against three big men! Jones and Obert are six-six or better too."

"Their guards weren't small by a long shot either!"

"It isn't going to do any good crying over spilled milk. State doesn't have what it takes! Period! The only thing we've got is Hilton."

"He'll help but—"

"That's right, *but!*"

"It's only the first game," a weak voice ventured. "Corrigan might still turn up something."

"Yeah," someone agreed loudly. "And that 'something' had better be a 'someone' like that big guy sitting down there beside Hilton."

The voices gradually died away as Assembly Hall emptied, but Chip and Branch remained in their seats. Neither had said a word since the end of the game. Branch Phillips was still studying the program, and Chip was trying to figure out how State could have gotten off to a better start.

There was no way, however. Not without a big man. He turned and grasped Branch gently by the arm. "Now I guess you know why I asked you to come to the game," he said.

Phillips nodded.

"And I guess you know what I'm going to ask you."

Again, he nodded.

"Well," Chip continued, "how about it? How about coming out for the team?"

CHAPTER 5

Character Counts

BRANCH PHILLIPS laced the long fingers of his hands together and cleared his throat nervously. "I wish I could, Chip. I'm a junior though, and by the time I got so I could do the team some good, I would be graduating. Or at least my eligibility would be over."

"You're good enough to help the team right now, Branch."

"But I haven't had any experience at all in college basketball."

"All you need is confidence."

"Maybe so, Chip, but I couldn't hold a player like Henninger."

"How do you know?"

"Well, I don't really *know*—"

"But I *do* know," Chip replied steadily, his gray eyes firm and direct. "You're a good shot and you can jump. That's plenty to start with."

"There's more to basketball than shooting and jumping, Chip."

"That's right. And you can do more than shoot and jump.

You can move and you learn fast, and that means you can be a good defensive player and a good rebounder. And that's just what we need—a tall player who can guard the other team's big man and get the ball off the backboards. That's our only weakness!"

"I'd love to play, Chip," Phillips said earnestly, looking down at the program he was twisting in his big hands, "especially if you think I could help the team. But even if I was good enough, I couldn't play."

"Why not?"

"Well, I told you about my father and about the money we had to borrow so I could finish the year at Southwestern. But that isn't all there is to it. You see, Chip, besides my mother, I have three sisters at home. The money I make at the Y helps with my school expenses, but it isn't enough to help at home. So I take care of the tree farm and the firewood route Pop built up."

"Firewood route?"

Phillips nodded. "I told you about the farm; it's the reason I'm going to forestry school. My grandfather got the place started, and Pop planted hundreds and hundreds of seedlings—"

"Seedlings?"

Branch grinned. "Small trees, Chip. Anyway, Pop started them a long time ago, and, well, I've been taking care of them. You see, the trees get more valuable every year. So, to keep us going until he could sell the trees, Pop started a firewood route. He used to cut up the prunings and the fallen timber and limbs for firewood and sell it to the people here in University. Some of the craft shops and florists also want the small pine branches—the prunings—to make decorative wreaths. Anyway, he built up a good, steady route, and I'm keeping it going."

"When do you find time to do all that?"

Phillips shrugged. "I find time. In the evenings after I finish at the Y and on Saturdays and Sundays too."

"When do you work the route?"

"Every morning before school. I load the firewood on the truck the last thing at night and then I get up at five o'clock the next morning and deliver it. That way I get finished before my first class."

"How often do you do that?"

"Six days a week."

Chip was stopped cold. He often felt tired from his daily combination of study, work, and athletics. But compared to Branch's schedule, his life was uncomplicated.

"I don't make much on the firewood and craft market, Chip," Phillips continued, "but it keeps things going at home. At Christmas time, we also have some trees available for the local stores. We'll be all right in a few years when most of the tree crop is ready for harvesting. Some of our farm timber is almost ready to sell. Right now, though, it's pretty tough."

"When do you study?"

Phillips grimaced. "That's another thing. I don't get much time to study, and I'm not doing too well with the books. Luckily, the work I've done on the farm helps with my forestry course."

Chip shook his head in admiration. His job at Grayson's was a snap. And five o'clock in the morning! Even Soapy would back away from that.

"Would a scholarship help, Branch? Tuition, fees, and board and room? I'm sure Coach Corrigan could look into it. When Bill King announced his plans to try out for the NBA, that might have opened up a spot for one."

"No, Chip, I get my meals at the Y and a small salary. Besides, my tuition is paid. It isn't very much. No, a scholarship wouldn't really help the family. I have to earn money to take home. Then, too, varsity basketball would take a lot of time—what with practices and games and traveling and all—and we just can't afford to lose our firewood route money and the craft store business."

He shook his head ruefully. "I sure hate to say no, Chip,

but there isn't anything else I can say. Pop never had much money, but he always said the firewood would put me through college and then he would have the timber left to take care of Mom and the girls. That's what it's going to do, but that doesn't leave me time for basketball."

"How about the timber? How long before you can sell that?"

"A lot of the trees take twenty-five years to reach maturity and be harvested. Some of it's pretty good right now, Chip, but I wouldn't think of selling the best growth for another five years. By that time, my sisters will be in high school and thinking about college. No, Chip, it looks as if I'll have to forget college basketball."

"Did you ever think about professional basketball?"

Phillips nodded. "Yes, I have. But I know I'm not ready. I need a lot of game experience and some good coaching, the kind of coaching I got from you this afternoon. When I went to Southwestern, I was hoping I could give professional basketball a try—after I got through college, that is. Now it looks as if I'll never get the chance."

"You never can tell, Branch. I have to work pretty hard to get through college, too, but you work a whole lot harder. You deserve a lot of credit. A person like you can do anything he sets his mind to." Chip paused reflectively. "If only there were a way for you to get some college coaching."

There was a short silence, and then Branch resumed the conversation. "I love basketball," he said wistfully. "I wish you could work with me every day." He paused and then added, "For a couple of months anyway."

"Maybe I can," Chip said quickly. "We can work in the afternoon next Monday, Tuesday, and Wednesday. Then, after I start practicing in the afternoon with the varsity, we can work at night. Coach Corrigan stops practice at 5:30 and then I hustle down to Grayson's to help out during the rush hour before I go out to get a bite to eat. You're free around seven o'clock, aren't you?"

Phillips nodded eagerly. "Sure! My job at the Y ends at six o'clock. It just means I'll get home a little later. But how about your dinner?"

"I don't really eat until around ten o'clock," Chip explained. "Most of the time I come here to shoot around a little. OK?"

"Great! I'm ready to give it a try!"

"It's a deal then. We'll work in the afternoons until Thursday and then we'll start our dinner-hour practice. All right with you?"

"What do you think?" Phillips said, grinning.

Assembly Hall was practically empty. Chip led the way to the exit. At the door he turned to look back at the darkened scoreboard. The big numbers 96 and 70 were still visible. He shook his head and moved on with his new friend beside him.

Branch had parked his truck behind the Y, and Chip walked along with him as they talked about the game. They shook hands and said good night when they reached the parking lot. Chip waited until Branch started the truck and drove away before he set out for Pete's restaurant.

Branch Phillips was big physically, all right, but more importantly, he was big in other ways. Chip hadn't met many people who would have had the determination and perseverance to stick to such a demanding program.

Soapy's sharp blue eyes spotted Chip as soon as he walked through Pete's front door. The redhead was sitting with Speed, Fireball, and Whitty in their regular booth, and he couldn't wait for Chip to sit down.

"What happened?" he called excitedly. "Is he gonna play? Are we gonna have a big man?"

Chip withheld the answer until he could slide into the booth beside Fireball and Whitty. "Branch has a lot of responsibilities, Soapy."

The hopeful expression faded from Soapy's face. "You mean he can't play?"

"It doesn't look like it."

"You look discouraged," Fireball observed. "You're not giving up, are you?"

"That's a silly question," Soapy accused. "Of course Chip isn't giving up. We've *got* to have this Phillips. He's our only chance for a good team."

Chip didn't say anything, but he was doing a lot of thinking. He glanced at the clock. It was five minutes after ten. Soapy was dead right. He sure wasn't giving up. "I think I'll stop by the Rock's house for a couple minutes," he said. "I'll meet you back at the dorm."

He walked swiftly up Tenth Street to Main and then took the shortcut across town, which passed by the Rockwell residence on the way to the campus.

As he walked, Chip thought about all the times he had turned to Coach Rockwell when he ran into some sort of crisis. The Rock was that sort of man, almost like a father to him. Chip knew all coaches weren't like the Rock, but he sure wished they could be. If he ever got to be a coach, he hoped he would be the same kind of strong leader that people could rely on.

He turned up the walk leading to the pretty red-brick colonial house. As he approached the house, he could see the Rock and Mrs. Rockwell sitting in front of a television set in the living room. Mrs. Rockwell opened the door almost as soon as he released the knocker. "Chip," she said, smiling fondly, "this is a surprise! Actually, I take that back. We saw you at the game, and Henry said he thought you would drop in tonight. Go right in and sit down. I'll get some milk and cookies. Oh, and congratulations on being elected captain!"

Henry Rockwell met him at the door of the living room and led him to a seat. "The same goes for me, Chipper. Here! Sit down."

"I don't want to take you away from your TV show, Coach."

Rockwell waved aside Chip's protests and snapped off the set. "I can watch television any time."

The conversation immediately centered on the game, and they were still discussing it when Mrs. Rockwell returned with refreshments. A little while later Chip told them all about Branch Phillips.

"I've heard about him, and he sounds like the answer to the team's problem," Rockwell said thoughtfully. "But from the point of financial aid, he isn't eligible for any help from the university other than the usual scholarship based upon need. His need for scholarship help is obvious, of course, but when it comes to financial help for his family there is nothing the school or anyone else can do. And you know the NCAA rules don't allow financial help for his family." He shook his head and continued. "I don't see how you can do anything more, Chip."

"Would it be all right for Mr. Grayson to help him? I mean, could he lend Branch some money for his family?"

"No, Chip. That would be evading the principle. It looks to me as if the decision is up to Branch Phillips and his mom."

"They're having a pretty hard time, I guess."

"But basketball isn't everything, Chip."

"I know that, Coach," Chip said slowly. "It's just that we were thinking about the Holiday Invitational. We'd like to win it for Coach Corrigan."

"It would be a nice send-off."

Chip nodded. "That's right. Besides, we don't like some of the things University fans are saying about him."

"A coach is no better than his players."

"Lots of people don't seem to realize that."

"The people who count know—President Babcock, Dean Murray, Dad Young, Curly Ralston, and everyone of consequence here at school. It's no disgrace to lose."

"Some of the students are blaming Coach Corrigan too," Chip said slowly.

"That's not unusual," Rockwell said wryly. "Most of us are used to that. It goes with the territory."

"I know, Coach, but it ought to be all right if we try to help."

Rockwell nodded understandingly. "I would be disappointed if you didn't. But I don't know what more you can do."

Chip smiled ruefully and got to his feet. "Well," he said, "it's getting late and I still have some studying to do, so I'll say good night. Thanks for your time, and the cookies, too, Mrs. Rockwell." He gathered his coat and headed for the door after shaking the Rock's hand.

When he reached his dorm, Jefferson Hall, Soapy and Speed were studying in the lounge on the first floor. Soapy looked up just as he paused in the doorway. The redhead nudged Speed and jerked his head toward Chip. They gathered up their books and joined him in the hall.

"Well?" Soapy queried, eyeing Chip quizzically.

"No luck, Soapy."

"Rock usually has the answer," Speed suggested hopefully.

"Not this time."

"You mean the school can't do anything?" Soapy asked indignantly. "Man, Chip, you don't have a scholarship. You're working your way! Why can't they double up on a scholarship for Phillips?"

"Because it's against the NCAA rules. It isn't right."

"Well," Soapy grumbled, "in this case it's all wrong."

Speed shuffled his feet worriedly. "What are we going to do, Chip?"

"Call a meeting!"

"What kind of meeting?" Speed asked.

"You know what kind!" Soapy said quickly. "A meeting of the strategy board—Biggie and Fireball and Red and Whitty and you and me—that's who!" Soapy turned and dashed for the steps leading to the second floor. "I'll get 'em, Chip. In our room, right?"

CHAPTER 6

Soapy's
Merry Men

SOAPY SMITH snapped off the overhead light and yawned deeply as he fumbled his way to his bed. "Oh, brother!" he moaned. "I'm dead tired. This night life is getting me down."

Chip didn't say anything, but he agreed with Soapy. If he didn't get Branch Phillips straightened out pretty soon he would be a mile behind in his studies. At least tomorrow was Sunday. He sighed with relief. He'd catch up on schoolwork then. If all the things he and his friends had planned during the past hour worked out, Branch Phillips's basketball problem was solved and Coach Corrigan's big-man troubles were over too.

Monday was a long day, despite the fact that Chip enjoyed his studies. When his classes ended at last, he hustled down to the University YMCA. But Branch hadn't arrived yet. Chip sat down in the lobby and glanced at the clock above the desk. It was fifteen minutes after three, and it didn't seem possible that it had been only a few short minutes since he had heard the first chime of the clock in the student union tower. His philosophy professor had decisively closed his antique pocket watch then and dismissed the class.

As they say in the army, Chip was thinking, it had been "hurry up and wait" all day! Soapy had been up that morning before the first weak ray of light spilled through their dormitory window. Chip woke up to Soapy whistling an off-key interpretation of State's "Victory March," and that had started it all off.

It had been wait for breakfast, wait for his first class, wait for the second, sit through a four-hour study period in the library, and then wait through his philosophy class. Now it was time to wait again! Anyway, he reflected, it was worth it. In a few minutes he would know whether Branch would be State University's first seven-foot center.

He had scarcely completed the thought when Branch arrived, brushing snowflakes from his coat. He saw Chip, and his long strides quickly carried him over to Chip's side.

"Sorry I'm late, Chip. I couldn't help it. I got held up by a field trip."

Chip motioned to a chair and Phillips sat down. "I'm tired," Chip's new big friend said, sighing. "I get enough field trips at home." He relaxed a moment and then added quickly, "I'm not too tired to practice though."

"Wait a minute," Chip said. "Branch, I think I've come up with a way for you to play basketball and still handle your firewood route. Sound good to you?"

Phillips nodded uncertainly. "Well, yes, of course, Chip. It sounds good, but I don't know how it can be done."

"There's a way," Chip said quietly. "Now let me ask you a few questions. All right?"

Branch nodded seriously. "Sure. Go ahead."

"All right. Number one, what's the toughest job connected with your firewood business?"

Phillips laughed. "That's easy! Cutting the wood."

"How do you cut it? Do you use an ax or a saw or *what!*"

"Well," Phillips explained, "I cut some of it with an ax and some with an ordinary wood saw and a lot of it with a power saw."

"How long does it take you to cut enough wood to keep up with the route? On a daily basis?"

Branch deliberated briefly. "I work every night until dark hauling logs and big limbs up near the barn where we have an outdoor light. Then I work under the light until I have enough firewood to fill the next day's orders."

"How many hours would that be?"

"I guess it would average about three hours on weekdays, half a day on Saturdays, and all day Sundays after we get back from church. That doesn't count the time it takes to make the deliveries, of course."

"Then it's a cinch!"

"What's a cinch? I don't understand."

"It's simple enough. My hometown friends from Valley Falls and some of the football guys have volunteered to do the hauling and cutting. We had a meeting Saturday night, and they're all for it. The football players are especially interested as they need the exercise to keep from getting out of shape. What do you think?"

"It's hard work, Chip, and it can be dangerous. Besides, Mom and I couldn't pay them very much."

"You don't know my friends, Branch. They don't want money. They want to help the team and you too! Biggie Cohen is six-four and weighs 240 pounds. Whitty Whittemore is as tall and nearly as heavy. Fireball Finley is as strong as a bull. He weighs more than two hundred pounds, and there are half a dozen others just as big. Don't worry about the danger either. A couple of them grew up on farms, and most of them have spent at least some time on a relative's farm. Of course, they wouldn't mind a couple of home-cooked meals on Saturdays and Sundays."

Branch grinned. "There isn't anyone who can cook better than my mom," he said proudly.

Chip could see Branch was impressed. "Well, then, what do you say?"

Phillips shook his head doubtfully. "I'll have to talk to Mom about it first," he said slowly.

Chip nodded, "Of course. Sure. But how do *you* feel about the idea?"

"I'd like to give it a try."

"Good! Now let's do some work."

They dressed quickly in the locker room and then hurried out on the court. Chip set the pace, starting close under the basket with layup shots and then working his way back to the free-throw line. He noted with pride that his new friend hadn't forgotten their first day's practice pointers. Branch was leaping high in the air before releasing the ball on his jump shots, utilizing every inch of his height. And he was hitting!

"This is great, Chip," Phillips said happily. "I've learned more basketball Saturday and today than I did all the time I was at Southwestern."

Branch's agility and quick learning curve thrilled Chip. His mind held no doubt about his friend's ability to help the team off the backboards. Everything depended upon Mrs. Phillips now.

Chip was so engrossed in the big player's progress that he forgot all about the time. And when the youngsters arrived and lined up on the side of the court, he couldn't believe it was already a little after four o'clock. "I guess that's it, Branch," Chip said, firing a final shot. "See you tomorrow afternoon. Same time."

He had scarcely finished the sentence when the kids surrounded him, holding up pens and slips of paper and clamoring for his autograph. Five minutes later he was in the shower.

It was just 4:30 when he arrived at Grayson's. Soapy had no customers and followed Chip back to the stockroom. "Was it all right?" he asked eagerly.

"He likes the idea. He's going to talk it over with his mom tonight and let me know tomorrow afternoon."

Soapy thought it over a moment. "I don't like it," he said, wrinkling up his freckle-laden nose. "Why don't we go out there and talk to Mrs. Phillips ourselves?"

Chip shook his head. "It's a family matter, Soapy. Besides, I don't even know where they live."

Soapy hooked a thumb over his shoulder. "Let's check the phone book!" he said suggestively.

"No," Chip said more firmly, "we should wait until tomorrow. If he's supposed to be on the team, it'll work out, right?"

Soapy nodded slowly. "I sure hope it does!"

The evening passed slowly. Despite having a stack of inventory invoices to input on the computer, Chip's thoughts turned again and again to Branch Phillips. Back in his dorm room at Jefferson Hall, Chip tossed and turned restlessly all through the long night. And the next morning every class seemed endless. He felt as though the afternoon would never come. All through the waiting, he kept telling himself that the only answer, the best answer, had to be yes.

But when he met Branch at the Y that afternoon, his friend's face told him the opposite.

Branch shook his head glumly. "I'm sorry, Chip. Mom doesn't think it will work. Besides, she said it wouldn't be fair to your friends."

"But they *want* to do it! They would do anything to help the team."

"Mom doesn't understand that, Chip." He groped for the right words. "She—well, she doesn't think work and play mix. Besides, she's pretty independent."

"Do you think it would help if I talked to her?"

"No, Chip, I don't think so. Besides being independent, she's pretty stubborn. When she makes up her mind, that's it!"

Chip dropped the matter and tried to conceal his disappointment by putting Branch through a hard workout.

But it was tough going, and it required a lot of effort to keep smiling when he left for Grayson's. His steps dragged as he thought ahead to Soapy's response. Chip was pretty sure how his friend would react. He could already hear the protest: "What kind of a woman is this Mrs. Phillips? I'll go see her myself!"

When Chip reached the large store, he glanced quickly at the fountain. Soapy wasn't at his usual station behind the old-fashioned soda counter. Chip sighed with relief and continued on into the store, pausing at the cashier's desk to talk with Mitzi Savrill. The petite beauty greeted him cheerily. "It won't be long now, Chip," she said brightly. "Only two more days."

"I wish I could play tomorrow night."

"Well, don't worry, Chip. It's a long season. There's plenty of time left."

Chip nodded and headed to the stockroom where Skip Miller was busy at work. Chip entered so quietly that he startled the young high school star. Skip turned quickly to see Chip standing just inside the door.

"Hey, Chip!" he said. "Glad you're here!" The surprised expression on his face turned to concern. "What's the matter? You all right?"

Chip smiled. "Sure, I'm all right. Just a little tired, that's all."

"Were ya working with Phillips at the Y?"

"That's right."

"What happened? Is he going to play?"

"It doesn't look like it."

"No wonder you look so down. Wait until Soapy hears about it. He'll go ballistic!"

Chip nodded and began to organize the orders on his desk. But something Skip had said struck a chord, and he dropped down in the chair to think it through. Now he had it! Soapy *would* go ballistic, he thought grimly. There was no way he would take no for an answer. That irrepressible redhead would want to charge straight out to the Phillips farm.

Wait a minute. What would be so bad about that? Soapy was a master salesman. He might be just the ticket to sell Mrs. Phillips on the idea of Branch playing basketball. Sure, that was it! If anyone could convince Mrs. Phillips, it was certain to be Soapy Smith!

Chip was still sitting in front of the computer when Soapy barged through the stockroom door. Soapy's weather-reddened cheeks matched his flaming red hair, which was tousled from the wind. The chill of the wintry outdoors followed him.

"I ran all the way from my last class," Soapy managed between gasps. "Man!" He paused to catch his breath, eyeing Chip expectantly as he took several deep breaths. "Well," he said with a final sigh, "any progress?"

"Maybe. I need your help."

"You got it. What?"

"Can you get Biggie and Whitty and Red and Fireball to go out to the Phillips farm with you tomorrow afternoon?"

Soapy nodded quickly. "Sure! Either Whitty or Fireball will have to work though. One's got to cover the fountain." Soapy paused and eyed Chip keenly. "Why? Is Phillips going to give us a try as woodsmen?"

"Mrs. Phillips might," Chip said. "Remember, I said *might*." Chip paused and then continued cryptically, "Unless I've overrated your sales ability all these years."

Soapy stood straighter and puffed out his chest. "No one's ever overrated me," he declared expansively. "What's your problem, my friend?"

"Selling Mrs. Phillips on the plan—you know, convincing her that the members of the strategy board can cut wood."

"That's no problem. Wait until she sees Biggie and Fireball and Red and some of the rest of the football players. We'll chop more wood in an hour than Branch Phillips can chop in a full week."

"It isn't that easy. She may not let you do anything."

"Why not?"

Chip then told Soapy about his conversation with Branch. As he talked, Chip could see Soapy's jaw set in firm lines, and he smiled inwardly. The redhead was a fun-loving and easygoing guy until the chips were down. Then he was all business and dead serious. Mrs. Phillips was in for a surprise.

When he finished, Soapy nodded and grinned. "I'll sell her on our idea! Just one thing—is Branch really good enough to help the team?"

"He sure is! If you can sell Mrs. Phillips on the idea, we'll have a good team. Maybe a great one."

Soapy smacked his right fist into the palm of his left hand. "That does it!" he said. "What's the plan now?"

"Branch and I are going to practice tomorrow afternoon at the Y again, and then he's promised to go to the game. While we're practicing, it's up to you to get out to the farm and convince Mrs. Phillips she ought to give you and the guys a chance to prove you can do the work. All right?"

Soapy nodded decisively. "You can count on that! Don't worry about a thing! I'll take care of Mrs. Phillips. Let's see, I've got to borrow a car and find out how to get there. Don't worry, Chip, there's nothing to it!"

"I'll believe that when I see Branch Phillips in a State University basketball uniform."

Soapy rubbed his hands together and grinned confidently. "It's practically done, my lad! Leave it to little ole Soapy and his merry woodsmen. We'll be at the Phillips farm tomorrow afternoon, rain or shine, snow or sleet, ice or . . . ice cream!" He bowed low. "Now if it pleases you, Sir Robin Hood, I'll get busy and line up my merry men."

CHAPTER 7

Around
the Clock

CATHEDRAL UNIVERSITY had two big men, but one would have been enough. When the visitors got the ball, their backcourt players would advance slowly toward the basket to give their big men time to get set. Then the smaller men would maneuver and move the ball until they could make a good pass to one of the giants for two and, more often, three points!

On the defense, Cathedral was using a zany zone. Chip couldn't figure out whether it was a one-three-one, a two-one-two, or a combination of both. Whatever it was, it was getting results.

His State University teammates were getting few outside shots because of the rushing tactics of the visitors' chasers, and every time Jimmy Chung or Bitsy Reardon drove in for a shot close to the basket, the big board men slammed the ball down their throats. The only way they could get a shot away was to start a hard drive, stop, and then go up for a jumper. Even then, the tall rebounders often batted the ball away.

Coach Corrigan tried every strategy in the playbook. But nothing worked. When he tried the press, Cathedral's big men would start upcourt, stop, cut back, and receive a high pass far above the heads of Chung, Slater, Reardon, Di Santis, or Tucker. Then Cathedral's smaller men would cut past the big men, take a handoff, and drive in for a quick score.

When Corrigan told the Statesmen to hold the ball and play possession, the visitors' chasers took chances, dove for the ball, and made all kinds of defensive errors, confident their big teammates would cover up the mistakes and get the ball.

Chip twisted and turned in his seat to watch the clock, praying for the end of the debacle. His only comforting thought was of Soapy and his other pals out at the Phillips farm. Every time he thought of them, he glanced sideways at Branch. Branch looked tense. His jaw was set grimly, and he moved his arms, legs, and body with every futile effort Chip's teammates made on the court. Like Chip himself, Branch was reaching for every pass, aiming every shot, trying for every rebound, and playing with all his heart for State.

Soapy should have been here by this time unless he had gone to work, Chip mused. Of course, the redhead and the other guys might still be chopping wood. He could imagine Soapy saying, "Aw, c'mon! Only one more log. What's with you guys? Tired? Look at the ole redhead. You gotta love it! Somebody's gonna get tired, but it isn't gonna be me!"

Soapy would give it all he had. And more! A sudden thought stopped his reverie. Perhaps Mrs. Phillips had been as adamant as Branch had said.

He glanced quickly at the scoreboard. The clock showed less than two minutes to play, with the visitors ahead by fifteen points. People were already leaving their seats, milling downward like a procession of ants. Chip looked up and around for the first time since the end of the first half. The tiered, bright red seats in Assembly Hall were nearly empty.

During the game he had closed his ears to the disappointed remarks of the fans sitting around him, just as he had closed them to the talk when he and Branch first came through the double doors and walked to the row of seats just behind the State bench.

Tomorrow, Soapy, Speed, and maybe a couple of the other guys from the football team would be out for practice. He would too. They would try to do something to help their teammates. Something more than just sitting in a seat on the sidelines and feeling frustrated. It was a lot to hope for, but maybe Branch would be out there too.

The buzzer sounded, ending the game, and Chip watched as the two teams' coaches shook hands. His teammates walked wearily to the locker room exit. He looked at the scoreboard and groaned. The score: Cathedral 61, State 46.

Chip was anxious to get down to Pete Thorpe's restaurant to find out how Soapy had made out. But Branch seemed lost in thought, and Chip waited for him to make the first move. After a minute or so, Phillips rose from his seat and grasped Chip's arm. "I'm sorry, Chip," he said slowly. "I really am. Now I see what you mean about needing a big man. But still, *you'll* be playing from now on, and maybe things will be different for State."

They walked slowly along the court to the nearest exit, both conscious of the attention they attracted. A number of fans called out friendly greetings to Chip. Most of them tried to cheer him up with encouraging words. A few of the more inquisitive directed their remarks toward Branch.

"That big guy in school?"

"Sure is! He's an ag student. Name's Phillips. He's a junior."

"Why isn't *he* out for the team?"

"Maybe he can't play basketball."

"Well, he's big enough to try, isn't he?"

"You got that right!"

The majority of spectators had departed, but small, scattered groups of fans stood around the lobby in front of the trophy cases, talking about the collapse of the Statesmen.

"This was supposed to be State's big year. If you ask me, State needs a new coach."

"You mean State needs some height."

"Well, anyway, Corrigan doesn't have to worry. He's taking a two-year sabbatical leave starting at the first of the year."

"Wonder who's getting the job?"

"I guess Rockwell will fill in for the rest of the season."

"I heard something about that guy from Northern State."

"I don't envy him the job."

"Well, starting Friday, we can watch the best player in the country. That's something anyway."

"Right! Too bad Hilton can't play with a good team. There's no telling how many points he might score."

Chip and Branch passed quickly through the lobby and out the wide exit into a cold, brisk wind. The parking lot, usually still jammed with traffic after a game, was nearly empty. Chip carried on a conversation with Branch as they walked toward the truck, but Chip's mind was busy with the complaints of sports fans. They sure couldn't stand a loser.

When the two friends reached Branch's truck, Chip waited until his tall friend drove away. Then he broke into a slow trot, his long legs eating up the distance as he swung behind the football stadium and along toward Pete's restaurant.

It was nearly eleven o'clock when Chip reached Grayson's. He slowed down and peered in as he passed by. The store was closed, so he hurried on around the corner, eager to join his friends. Just outside the restaurant he stopped and looked through the frosty window. Pete was standing in front of their usual booth. Chip knew they were there. He opened the door and smiled as he heard Soapy's voice.

The redhead was doing the talking, but he must have sensed Chip's presence. He stood up and waved to Chip over the top of the booth. "Hey, Chip!"

Chip could tell that Soapy was excited, and he hoped it was because of good news. A quick glance around showed Fireball, Whitty, Biggie, Red, and Speed in the gathering. "Well," he said, trying to speak calmly, "what happened?"

"Lots of things," Soapy said quickly. "We cut wood, piled it, bundled it, stacked it, ate dinner with the family, and—" he paused and eyed Chip triumphantly—"we got Mrs. Phillips to promise to come to the Carlton game Friday night! How about that!"

"That's fine, Soapy," Chip said slowly, "but how about Branch? Did she say he could play?"

Soapy shook his head, and his smile disappeared. "No, Chip, not exactly. But she did say she would think it over. I didn't really have much of a chance to get anything out of her."

"Only four servings of stew, four biscuits, and three pieces of apple pie," Speed added quickly, winking at Chip and elbowing Red Schwartz in the side.

"When you work, you gotta eat!" Soapy retorted, but he had the grace to blush a bit.

"What about the wood cutting?" Chip persisted. "Did she think we could do the job?"

"She thought we could do the job just fine," Red said proudly. "You should have seen Biggie and Fireball handle the axes."

"We convinced her," Soapy said smugly.

"Not as much as you think," Biggie said quietly, shaking his head. His voice was serious and thoughtful. "Mrs. Phillips is an unusual woman. I think she would let Branch play in a minute if she knew how to pay us for the work. But they don't make very much money, only about thirty dollars, I think, for one of the bundles, and they sell only so many."

Chip tried to conceal his disappointment. "Branch said his mother wouldn't understand—"

"Don't worry, Chipper," Soapy said quickly. "We've made the first big step. Mrs. Phillips has never seen a college basketball game. Wait until she sees *you* play."

"Yeah!" Red added. "And wait until you see *her!*"

"I think she just wanted some time to think about it," Fireball added. "We've got to convince her that we feel strongly enough about the school and the team to make such a sacrifice."

"Speaking of teams," Speed observed dryly, pointedly looking at his watch, "we're reporting for practice tomorrow. Remember?"

Their meeting ended and they headed out for Jeff. The cold wind was too strong for much talking, but Chip did answer their questions about the game, and once again they discussed the inability of the team to cope with the big men. When they reached the second floor of Jeff, they all said good night. Chip and Soapy headed into 212 while the others trudged down the hall to their own dorm rooms.

Soapy was dead tired, and it seemed to Chip that he was asleep and snoring five minutes after he hit his bed. It took Chip a little longer. He was thinking about the team and his first practice the next afternoon. It would be great to work out with the guys once again.

He was the first player to report for practice the next afternoon. Murph Kelly was in a bad mood and grumbling to himself, but he brightened when he saw Chip. "This is the worst basketball team State's had in ten years, Hilton," he said gruffly. "Maybe you can put a little punch into the offense. So far, Coach hasn't found anyone who can get him some points."

After Chip was dressed, Kelly walked over to the ball bin and picked out a new ball. "Here!" he said, tossing the ball to Chip. "Get out of here and sharpen up your shooting eye."

Chip started with a tap-in drill under the basket and was hard at it when Soapy and Speed joined him. They immediately challenged him to a shooting contest. Each had a good eye for the basket and gave Chip a run for it at first. Then his superior marksmanship began to tell, and he hit ten straight.

"Lucky!" Soapy said shortly.

"It's the ball," Chip said, laughing at Soapy's discomfort. "I own it!"

A few minutes later Jimmy Chung, J. C. Tucker, and Bitsy Reardon came hustling up to welcome him. Then the rest of the squad appeared, and Coach Corrigan blasted his whistle and yelled for his three-lane drill. Chip was raring to go. The whole team caught fire, yelling and cheering each play. Two hours later the coach called it a day and sent the team to the bleachers.

When the players quieted, Corrigan cleared his throat nervously before speaking. "Men," he said slowly, "about the toughest thing a coach has to do is cut the squad. But it's part of the job and has to be done. So, after you shower and dress, you'll find the list of players who will dress for the Carlton game tomorrow night posted on my office door.

"We sincerely thank everyone for coming out for the team. If you've been cut, we hope you'll try out again next season. The rest of you should be prepared to leave for Southern tomorrow night right after the Carlton game. That's all." He turned away, and the players quietly made their way to the locker room. Chip waited for Soapy and Speed.

"I'll never make it, Chip," Soapy groaned. "Not after only one day of practice! I don't think Coach even saw me!"

"He saw you," Chip said confidently. "And he knows what you can do. Besides, you're in shape."

Speed elbowed Soapy and snickered. "Man, some shape!"

Soapy turned toward Speed belligerently, his troubles forgotten for the moment. "Sure I'm in shape," he said, pounding his chest with his fists. "I'm as hard as a rock!"

"You'll make it, Soapy," Speed said, grinning as he darted for the locker room door.

Soapy's wide smile followed Speed's departing figure. Then, serious again, he walked slowly beside Chip. He was still worried, but he pretended it wasn't important. The three of them took their time showering and dressing, and when they walked up the ramp to Coach Corrigan's office above the gym, the hall was empty.

Soapy held back. "I can't look," he said. "Someone tell me. Quick!"

Speed read the names. "Hilton, Di Santis, Tucker, Chung, Reardon, Morris, Slater, Williams, Hunter, Freedman, Hicks, and—Smith!"

"No!" Soapy gasped.

"Yes!" Speed said happily. "I told you, didn't I?"

"Wow! Oh, wow!" Soapy declared. "Well, I was last, but—"

"Better last than never," Chip interrupted brightly. "Come on! We're late."

They walked briskly across the campus and down Main Street to Grayson's. Chip worked until a few minutes before seven and then started out for the Y. He found Branch Phillips working all alone in the gym when he arrived.

Phillips grinned at Chip and said, "Hiya, Chip. Watch this!"

He dribbled hard under the basket, leaped high in the air, buttonhooked with a twist of his body, and zipped the ball down through the hoop with his right hand. He retrieved the ball, dribbled away from the basket, circled back, and did the same thing with his left hand.

Chip nodded in admiration. "That's great, Branch."

"I've been practicing it for the past hour," Branch said proudly. "Chip, I have to tell you, Mom thinks the guys are great. She invited them all back for dinner this Sunday. You're invited too. I'll meet you at Assembly Hall when you get back from the Southern game."

He paused to catch his breath and continued quickly, "You'll come, won't you?"

"I'll be there."

Phillips beamed. "That's good. Mom wants to meet you."

"Soapy says she's coming to the game tomorrow night."

"That's right. She's never been to a basketball game."

"Not even when you played?"

Phillips shook his head vigorously. "No, never!"

"What about tomorrow night? What changed her mind?"

Branch shook his head and grinned widely. "I guess you know Soapy Smith."

"As well as anyone, I guess."

"Well, Mom thinks he's the greatest. I don't know how he ever got her to promise to come to the game, but she's sure coming!"

CHAPTER 8

"It's a Shame"

COACH CORRIGAN was walking back and forth across the width of the locker room, pausing now and then to look at the white board. Earlier, he had written the names of the Carlton players on the board. Opposite each name, matched as closely as possible according to size and skills, were the names of three of State's starting five. Two places remained open. Chip studied the board.

> *Campbell* (#13) 6-4; 180 ——————— *Hilton*
> Fast. Jump shot. (20 points)
> Lefty. Overshift to right.
>
> *Green* (#35) 6-4; 200 ——————
> Strong. Follow-in. (12 points)
> Poor defense. Righty.
>
> *Stanton* (#5) 6-10; 230 ——————— *Di Santis*
> Pivot shots. Good. (31 points)
> Strong defense. Righty.
> Tap-in shots. Tough.

Gregory (#14) 6-1; 170 ———————— *Chung*
Playmaker. Two-hand set. (9 points)
Leads fast break. Intercepts.
Righty.

Kalish (#11) 6-3; 190 ————————
Good defense. Takes charge. (4 points)
Seldom cuts. Good rebounder. Lefty.
Makes outlet pass for fast break.

Chip concentrated on Campbell's description. "Fast," he mused. "Same size and averaging twenty points a game. Jump-shooter. I'll keep to his right when he has the ball and make him go to my left."

He shifted his attention to number 5, Carlton's big center. Six-ten, 230. Averaging thirty-one points a game. Di Santis had a big job ahead of him. Gregory was Jimmy Chung's opponent. He was six-one, weighed 170, and was the playmaker and the leader of Carlton's fast break. Well, Jimmy would take care of him in short order.

Corrigan moved swiftly to the board and wrote *Reardon* opposite *Kalish*. Then he wrote *Tucker* opposite Carlton's *Green*. "That's it!" he said, facing the players. "That's the way we start."

There wasn't a sound for a long moment. Then Corrigan turned toward Murph Kelly, who was standing quietly beside a training table. "Give me a ball, Murph."

Kelly tossed the coach a ball, and Corrigan handed it to Chip. Then he extended his hand. "All right, men," he said quietly. "Let's go!"

Seconds later, Chip led his teammates through the locker room door and out to the players' ramp. The Carlton players were already on the floor, and a quick glance around the arena showed that Assembly Hall was jammed, and jamming! The home and visiting crowds were up for this game!

Followed by his teammates, Chip stepped out onto the court and dribbled toward the State University basket. A tremendous outburst broke from the seats and grew in intensity as the team, dressed in State University's bright white and red, sprinted upcourt to start Corrigan's three-lane warm-up drill.

Chip passed to Jimmy Chung and followed in to take the rebound. Then he whipped the ball to Di Santis and trotted up the side of the court. As he neared the State bench, he saw Phillips in the second row of seats. Branch was watching him, and as soon as he caught Chip's eye, he pointed to the lady beside him. Chip knew instantly it was Branch's mom. He stopped when he reached them and leaned across the front row of seats.

"This is my mother, Chip," Branch said proudly. Mrs. Phillips extended a long arm and grasped Chip's hand in a firm grip. "I'm glad to meet you, Chip Hilton," she said, smiling. "You're all I've heard about for the past week, along with State University basketball."

Chip could see where Branch got his height. Even though she remained seated, he could see Mrs. Phillips was exceptionally tall. She had a fair complexion; a long, straight nose; and steady brown eyes. Her short brown hair was touched with gray.

"I'm glad to meet you," Chip said. "Branch has been telling me a lot about you too. I've got to get back to my warm-up now. Will I see you after the game?"

"You will!" Branch said. "We'll wait for you. Right here!"

Chip hustled back into the drill. At the other end of the court, the Carlton players were going through their drill. The visiting crowd cheered every time a player swished a ball through the hoop. It was a tall team, Chip noted. He watched the opponents' elbows rise high above the rim with their rebounding efforts. They were a strong team.

"Y-e-a . . . State! Rah! Y-e-a-h . . . Go team! Fight!" The State University cheerleaders were cartwheeling across the floor, their skirts billowing like twirling umbrellas of red and white. Three male cheerleaders ran the length of the court waving huge crimson, blue, and white State banners. The spectators, proudly on their feet, joined in singing the State University fight song, shouting the last three syllables. "Go, SU!"

Chip pulled off his warm-up jacket and then took his turn on the free-throw line. He hit ten straight and felt a warm glow of satisfaction; he felt right and still had the touch.

"Atta boy, Chipper," Soapy cheered. "We'll kill 'em!"

The referee blasted his whistle, and the players of both teams walked toward the benches. Coach Corrigan was shifting nervously from one foot to the other as he waited for the players to surround him. Then Hilton, Di Santis, Chung, Tucker, and Reardon were ready, and Corrigan sent them out on the court.

"Go team! Fight, fight, fight!"

Stanton easily got the tap. His long arm reached far above Di Santis's desperate leap, and he deftly pushed the ball to Green. Chip had ignored the tap and was concentrating on Campbell. It was a good thing he did because his opponent broke for the Carlton basket a split second before Stanton tapped the ball. Even then, Campbell succeeded in getting a step on him.

Anticipating a long lead pass, Chip held his arms over his head and raced after the fleet scorer. Then, three strides in front of the Carlton basket, Chip saw Campbell's eyes flash upward. This was it!

Chip turned instantly, just in time to reach up and intercept Green's pass. Then, throwing a hard stop, he pivoted and dribbled upcourt, heading for the State University basket at full speed.

The State fans had been shocked by Stanton's easy control of the tap. But when Chip intercepted the ball, they recovered their confidence. Their cheers echoed among the rafters, and the roar of exultation continued as Chip drove upcourt. Kalish was waiting for him at the free-throw line, but up ahead Chip saw a white flash cutting under the basket. His lightning-fast bounce pass hit Jimmy Chung just right for a layup bank shot. Two points!

Kalish followed Chip's pass and tried desperately to stop Jimmy's shot. But he was too late. His leap did, however, permit him to whisk the ball out of the net. He landed out of bounds and turned to look upcourt. Then he fired a hard baseball pass up the side of the court to Campbell, who waited just beyond the ten-second line.

Chip groaned and sprinted for the Carlton basket. But Campbell had too much of a lead. The fleet forward dribbled to the outer half of the free-throw circle and threw a quick stop. Then he went up in the air for a jump shot. The spinning ball dropped cleanly through the hoop for Carlton's first tally.

Chip's mad pace had carried him close to Campbell, but not in time to stop the shot. He continued on and caught the ball before it hit the floor. As he stepped across the end line with the ball, he was thinking about the mistake he had made by not looking for Campbell when he had intercepted the ball. He should have passed to a teammate and located Campbell right away.

Coach had said to stick with Campbell, and he had fallen down on the job on the very first play! Campbell was a basket hanger, a scorer, and only interested in making points. Well, there would be no more of that.

Chip inbounded to Jimmy, who dribbled slowly up the right side of the court. Up ahead, the Carlton players moved to pick them up on a man-to-man basis according to the positions the players had taken for the center tap.

Kalish, towering over Jimmy, picked him up at the ten-second line. That was a mistake. Jimmy had room to maneuver, and after a slow change of pace, Chung opened up with dazzling dribbling speed and drove past his tall opponent as if he were standing still. For a second it looked as if Jimmy would have an easy layup. But just as the tall player called Henninger had done in the Wilson University game, Stanton darted away from Di Santis and batted the ball out of Jimmy's hand. Kalish grabbed the ball—and Carlton's fast break was underway.

Chip played Campbell hard-nose and dogged him every move he made, playing him so closely Campbell couldn't even get the ball. But it didn't matter. Someone passed the ball in to Stanton, and the big pivot star whirled and banked the ball against the backboard for the basket.

Bitsy dribbled slowly upcourt and then fed the ball to Di Santis, who had taken a high-post position. Chip cut behind Reardon and sped toward the basket. His sudden move gained a step on Campbell, and he took the ball from Dom at full speed.

Stanton left his defensive position behind Di Santis and attempted to stop Chip's shot. But he didn't get his hand on the ball this time. Chip faked the shot and then bounced the ball to Dom on the other side of the basket. Dom was all alone when he laid the ball against the backboard and into the basket to tie the score.

Carlton moved slowly to the attack, using its possession offense to move the ball until it could be passed to Stanton near the basket. Once again, Dom was unsuccessful in keeping the ball from Carlton's big center. Stanton whirled and dealt for the two-pointer.

State kept pace with Chip's jumper from the back of the circle. Then Carlton ran the score to 18-8 before Bitsy Reardon dropped in a baby-jumper from the side. Carlton got it right back when Green went up over J. C. Tucker's head to tap in the first shot Stanton had missed.

The State University home fans were clearly disturbed. Once again it was obvious that State could not cope with a big player. Chip was covering Campbell tightly and had held the visiting scoring star to a mere two points.

With State in possession, Corrigan stood up and called for a time-out. The Statesmen surrounded him in front of the bench. While Murph Kelly and the assistant trainers handed out towels and water bottles, Corrigan spoke rapidly. "We're not getting anywhere. We've got to change our plans."

"I can't hold Stanton, Coach," Di Santis said glumly. "I've got four personals and I haven't stopped him yet."

"We could try the press," Jimmy offered tentatively.

"Not yet," Corrigan said. "We'll save that for the second half."

"How about the one-three-one zone?" Reardon asked.

Corrigan shook his head. "No, that wouldn't help. We'll try something else. Chip, I want you to cut loose and get some points. On the defense, play Stanton. Tucker, you take Campbell. Dog him every step he makes. Dom, you take Green. OK?"

When time was in, Chip took the ball out of bounds and passed incourt to Jimmy. Then he cut along the sideline, fishhooked back, got a return pass from Jimmy, and scored with a twisting jumper that brought a tremendous cheer from the fans. Carlton came upcourt and started its slow-moving attack then, and Chip lined up in front of Stanton, playing between the big man and the ball.

Stanton cut out in front of Chip for a pass and tried a long three-point shot. But he was too far out, and the shot was too short and didn't reach the basket. Air ball!

Chip retreated, caught the ball high in the air, and passed it to Jimmy. The fiery little dribbler took off at full speed and drove down the middle of the court. After passing the ball, Chip cut up the sideline and outran Stanton. Sprinting swiftly toward the basket, he took Jimmy's pass and laid the ball over the rim and through the hoop for two. With Chip free to score, the Statesmen made up six of the ten-point deficit by the end of the half. The score: Carlton 41, State 37.

The second half developed into a one-man show. Di Santis, guarded by Stanton, inbounded the ball to Chip. The big pivot star swatted at the ball and got a piece of it, but Chip darted after it and pulled it in. Then he dribbled into the front court and sank a solid jumper.

Kalish took the ball out of bounds. Turning away, Chip played dummy. But when Kalish attempted to pass the ball to Green, Chip whirled, snared the ball, and dropped it in the basket to tie up the score, 41-41.

The fans were on their feet now, cheering the unexpected turn of the game. Seconds later, Chip stole a pass intended for Stanton and dribbled the length of the floor to score again. The basket put State in the lead, and the crowd went mad.

The wild pace continued into the fourth quarter and, with seven minutes to play, State was ahead 62-61. Chip had scored thirty-nine points. Carlton managed to slow down the pace and forge ahead during the next three minutes, chiefly because the Statesmen had run out of steam.

Chip could hardly move when Corrigan took him out of the game. There were four minutes left to play, and Carlton led by a single point, 72-71.

Speed replaced him, and Chip dropped thankfully down on the bench next to Coach Corrigan. He had played his heart out, and every muscle in his body ached. He had been so sure that he was in shape. But he had been far from ready for thirty-six minutes of this kind of basketball. Chip shook his head ruefully. Football training was rugged, all right, but basketball was different. A player never had a chance to stop. Especially when his team was using the full-court press.

The teams traded baskets, and then Di Santis fouled Stanton. It was his fifth personal. The referee informed a dejected Di Santis as he headed for the bench. Corrigan sent Rudy Slater into the game for Di Santis, and a second later Stanton sank the free throw and Corrigan called for a time-out.

Carlton was ahead 75-73. Chip was thrilled by the fight his teammates were putting up out on the court. They were dead tired too. He felt a sudden surge of power and determination and took several deep breaths. Using Kelly's relaxation formula of loosening his muscles and imagining they were pieces of tissue paper drifting down to the floor, Chip prayed he would be ready should Corrigan send him back into the game.

When time was in, Corrigan called for another time-out. The fans had quieted a little, and Chip heard Branch, sitting two rows behind the State bench, talking to his mother. "It isn't fair, Mom. Stanton is eight inches taller. It's a shame, that's what it is!"

CHAPTER 9

Every Inch of the Way

"WE WANT HILTON! We want Hilton! We want Hilton!"
The chant increased in volume and drowned out any further
conversation that Branch and Mrs. Phillips might have had.
Chip took several more deep breaths and glanced at the
scoreboard. With less than two minutes to go, Carlton was
ahead 75-73.

Corrigan left the player huddle and sat down beside him.
"How about it, Chip? Are you all right? I've used my last
time-out, so it's now or never."

"I'm all right, Coach. I can do it."

"Good! Report for Slater! Hurry!"

Every fan in Assembly Hall was watching the drama on
the bench, and a thunder of applause burst from the stands
when Chip stood up and shrugged off his State U warm-
ups. The cheers followed him as he walked to the scorers'
table to report. He hurried back to the huddle in front of the
bench and draped his arms around the shoulders of Speed
and J. C. Tucker.

Corrigan was speaking rapidly. "We've got to score *now*,

men. Right now! There's no time to lose and no time to play for one shot. We're two points down and time is running out. Thank goodness it's our ball.

"Jimmy, you take it out and pass in to Chip. Then the rest of you get out of the way and let Chip drive. If Stanton picks him up, Chip will go right by him. If Campbell plays him, Chip might be able to drive in for a three-point play.

"If we fail to score, go right into your man-to-man press. If we tie it up, drop back and play straight man-to-man. But don't foul. They'll try to hold the ball either way and play for one shot. Time's up now. Go get 'em!"

It was the smallest team Corrigan could have put on the court. It was up to Jimmy, Bitsy, Speed, J. C. Tucker, and himself. Anyway, it was a fast team and that was what was needed when using a full-court press. Chip had felt all right until he got up from the bench, but then the aches and pains returned, and he felt stiff and sluggish.

He cut back toward the Carlton basket, reversed, and leaped high in the air to receive Jimmy's pass. Dribbling to the right, he was surprised when Kalish, the visitors' star defensive player, picked him up and moved cautiously along between him and the basket. The Carlton coach had figured Corrigan would tell Chip to try for the score.

Chip passed to Speed and cut through, but Kalish was practically on top of him. Speed didn't have a chance to return the pass. The ball went from Speed to J. C. to Bitsy and back to Jimmy. Speed set a nice pick behind Kalish, but when Chip cut, he found the speedy guard still with him. Kalish had avoided the pick with a lightning-fast pivot. Chip felt a sharp pang of fear. Time was running out!

Jimmy dribbled across the court and set a pick on the left side of Kalish. Chip saw it coming, faked right, and then called on all his speed to cut around the dribbling wizard. But Jimmy's opponent stepped back, and Kalish slid through, and there he was again, in perfect defensive position between Chip and the basket.

Jimmy could have taken a shot when his opponent moved back to let Kalish through. Chip wished he had. There was less than a minute to go, and the Carlton players were playing a heads-up defensive game.

Jimmy bounced a pass to Speed and cut away from the ball. Speed gave Chip the ball and did likewise. Chip dribbled slowly to the right, then called on a burst of speed to drive toward the right sideline. Kalish was leeching him. Just when it looked as if the Carlton defensive star had him trapped, Chip slowed down. Continuing his slow pace, he moved forward and then suddenly dribbled behind his back in the other direction, then shifted the ball to his left hand, and drove hard for the basket.

Kalish was caught off balance for a split second. Chip had all the advantage he needed, a half step. He threw a hard stop just outside the free-throw circle and went up for a jump shot.

Stanton left Tucker and charged toward him. Kalish had caught up and he too sprang forward in an attempt to stop the shot. The three players converged at full speed and crashed together high in the air just as Chip released the ball. He was knocked to the polished hardwood floor, but even as he fell, he knew the ball had been deflected. Stanton and Kalish tumbled down on top of him, but they scrambled to their feet and then each extended a hand to lift Chip up.

Chip heard the blasting of the referee's whistle and saw the official point first to Stanton and then to Kalish. And he was holding a hand high above his head with two fingers extended.

Chip's heart leaped. A *multiple* foul! One on Stanton and one on Kalish. He had two shots coming. It was a chance to tie the score. His legs felt limp and lifeless, but he concealed the weakness as best he could and walked slowly toward the free-throw line. Just before he reached it, he stopped to take a deep breath and glanced at the scoreboard: Carlton 75, State 73. And only twenty seconds left to play.

The referee handed him the ball as he stepped up to the line. The crowd quieted. It was as though someone had snapped off a TV late at night. Chip bounced the ball on the floor and concentrated on the middle of the basket ring. Then he jiggled the ball lightly on his fingertips and snapped his shooting arm and hand upward and outward in a full follow-through. The ball went spinning lightly and accurately through the hoop and rocked once in the net before falling into the hands of the waiting official.

"One coming now," the referee called, holding the ball. "Remember! The ball is in play." He tossed the ball to Chip and stepped out of the lane.

Chip glanced once more at the scoreboard. Carlton 75, State 74. And there were still twenty seconds to go.

He got his line and judged the range and bounced the ball once. Then he snapped it out at the basket. But the shot was a trifle out of line. The ball hit the left side of the rim, bounced against the basket support, continued upward to hit the backboard, and then dropped through the hoop to tie up the score.

The State fans released a cheer of relief, but it promptly reverted to apprehension as Carlton's top scorer, Campbell, brought the ball swiftly upcourt.

"Hold 'em! Watch Campbell! Hold 'em, State!"

And from the Carlton section: "One shot! One shot!"

"Hold 'em, State! Fifteen seconds! Hold 'em!"

Kalish had played Chip on the free-throw line, but just as the ball fell through the basket, he and Green and Gregory dashed upcourt for the Carlton basket. Chip backtracked as fast as he could, determined to break up the attempt of the opponents to get a three-two situation on Jimmy and Bitsy, who were playing in the backcourt. He had planned to pick up Stanton and play him hard-nose, but there wasn't time. He had to stick with Kalish and leave Speed to play Campbell and Tucker to cover Stanton.

"Ten seconds! Ten seconds!"

Kalish cut under the basket, and Campbell fired the ball to him. But Chip was giving the Carlton guarding expert a dose of his own medicine, and Kalish was forced to pass out to Gregory. Then Chip saw Stanton cut down the opposite sideline to the corner and break out toward Gregory. Tucker was in a good guarding position, but he was a pygmy chasing a giant, and Gregory hit Stanton with a high pass.

The big pivot star never broke stride; he caught the ball at full speed and hooked it over his shoulder and high above Tucker's hand just as the buzzer sounded.

Chip automatically blocked Kalish and jockeyed for a good rebound position. Then he felt all the power and strength and hope go out of his arms and legs and heart as the ball kissed the backboard sweet and true and went spinning down through the hoop and through the net and into the hands of a Carlton player.

The game was over, and just that fast the big numbers on the scoreboard had recorded the score: Carlton 77, State 75.

Stanton hurried up to him, clasped his arm, and shook his hand. "Great, Hilton. You're *really* great. It was a tough one to lose."

"Congratulations, Stanton," Chip said earnestly, trying to smile.

He was trapped after that by the fans who evaded security and came pouring out on Corrigan's precious floor. They blocked Chip's path and patted him on the back and asked for autographs.

It took Chip five minutes to reach the State bench. Some of the team managers were talking to friends, and as he walked along the bench looking for his warm-up jacket, he noticed Branch and his mother were surrounded by fans. He found his jacket and heard a fan say, "Hilton may be an all-American, but Stanton outplayed him."

"Why shouldn't he?" Branch retorted hotly. "Stanton is nearly seven feet tall."

"How tall are you?" someone asked significantly. Branch made no reply, but another fan eagerly broke in to say, "Stanton gave them all a lesson. Corrigan and State and Hilton too."

Branch's voice was trembling with emotion, but it was bitterly precise. "You mean Chip Hilton gave fans like you a lesson. Stanton didn't outplay him. Chip scored forty-one points and nearly won the game. And when State lost, he never showed any poor sportsmanship. That's more than I can say about some of the poor losers I've been listening to here in the seats all evening."

"Quiet, Branch," Mrs. Phillips remonstrated.

"I can't help it, Mom," Branch said bitterly. "If only I had gone to State in the first place!"

"You're going now."

"I don't mean for school," Branch said stoutly. "I mean for *basketball.*"

Chip didn't hear any more of what passed between Branch and his mom, but he felt a warm glow of appreciation for Branch's loyalty. He made his way across the court to the players' ramp leading to the State locker room and then headed through the hall. Pausing to take a deep breath, he waited a moment and then opened the door.

Murph Kelly was checking the contents of his kit, keeping busy and muttering to himself, when Chip walked into the locker room. Speed and the rest of his teammates were sitting on the benches in front of their lockers, trying to relax. None of them had made a move to take off their uniforms. Coach Corrigan was standing in the center of the room looking steadily at the white board. Chip glanced quickly at his teammates' faces and dropped heavily down onto the bench next to Soapy in front of their lockers. There certainly wasn't much to cheer about, but the Statesmen were far from quitting. One could see the determination etched in their set jaws and the grim expressions on their faces.

"Nice game, Chip," Di Santis said in a low voice. "Sorry I couldn't hold him."

"He made the winning shot on me," Tucker said. "It was my fault."

"Just a second, men," Corrigan said gently, turning away from the white board to face his team. "If anyone is to blame, it's me. I should have had something special set up for Stanton. Every one of you, whether on the bench or in the game, gave all you had and then some! When you do that, it doesn't matter who wins!

"Sure I would have liked to see you win. You deserved the victory. But you did the next best thing. You fought every inch of the way with every bit of your beings. That's enough for me and for every real sportsman. I'm proud of you.

"We've lost three games in a row, but I predict right now that we're going to surprise a lot of people in the next three weeks." He paused and nodded grimly. "It wouldn't surprise me if we did a repeat of last year's Holiday Invitational. I'm sure you remember we won that one when no one thought we had a chance. Well, there's no reason we shouldn't win it this year, in Madison Square Garden!"

"Right!" Di Santis said aggressively. "That's the spirit, Coach!"

"And how!" Soapy said. "We'll annihil—oh, good grief! We'll kill 'em!"

Jim Corrigan nodded in approval and raised his hand for silence. "We'll sure try, Soapy. And we'll start with Southern tomorrow night." He looked at his watch and continued. "It's ten-seventeen, and our bus leaves for the airport at eleven." He turned to Andre Gilbert and smiled. "Let's get everything packed up. We're on our way."

The tension was broken now, and the locker-room chatter was soon back to normal. Chip dressed rapidly, remembering that Branch and his mother were waiting. Soapy and Speed kept pace. When the three friends reached the playing court, they walked around the highly polished surface and approached the bench.

Chip saw that Bill Bell, sports editor of the *Herald,* was talking to Branch. Then the sportswriter leaned over to say something to Mrs. Phillips. She nodded and stood up, and Chip almost stopped in his tracks. Mrs. Phillips was the tallest woman he had ever seen. She was several inches taller than Bill Bell, and he wasn't a small man by any means. Chip strode along in front of Soapy and Speed, and as he neared the little group, he heard Bell say, "What do you think about it, Mrs. Phillips?"

"Branch is old enough to make his own decisions, Mr. Bell. Frankly, I am opposed to it. But basketball seems to mean so much to him that I— Well, I won't stand in his way. The choice is up to him."

Chip slowed his pace and waited, his heart beating rapidly, as Bill Bell turned back to Branch.

"What about it, Phillips?" Bell asked. "Are you going to play?"

"I'm going to give it a try, Mr. Bell," Branch said firmly.

Soapy darted forward. "Branch!" he exploded. "You mean it?"

Phillips nodded. "I sure do!"

"And it's all right with you, Mrs. Phillips?" the redhead demanded.

"Yes," Mrs. Phillips said evenly. "If Branch can help the team and the coach wants him—"

"Wants him!" Soapy repeated excitedly. "Man, oh man!"

Soapy pivoted and dashed straight across the court. "I'll be right back!" he yelled over his shoulder. "I've gotta tell Corrigan. Oh, man! Will he be surprised!"

CHAPTER 10

A Big Man at Last

CHIP COULDN'T RESIST a wide grin when Coach Corrigan and Soapy appeared and strode speedily across State's expensive basketball court in their street shoes. The coach would have bawled out State's president, James Elmore Babcock, for doing the same thing.

Corrigan was breathing rapidly when Soapy introduced him to Mrs. Phillips. And he wasted no time in small talk. "If what Soapy tells me is true, Mrs. Phillips," he said breathlessly, "you're looking at a very happy man."

"It's true, Mr. Corrigan."

"Can he go with us tonight? We're leaving right away, in ten minutes."

"He can go."

"What about a uniform?" Chip asked.

"Right!" Corrigan said quickly. "Soapy! Tell Kelly to get Sky Bollinger's uniform from last year out of the equipment room. Hustle now!"

Soapy dashed across the court and Corrigan glanced down at Branch's feet. "Uh, oh," he said doubtfully. "What size shoes do you wear?"

"Nineteen, Coach."

"Nineteen," Corrigan repeated, shaking his head slowly from side to side. "That means they have to be specially ordered—that'll take a couple of weeks."

"No worries, sir. I have a pair at the Y," Phillips said.

Corrigan breathed a sigh of relief. "Great!" he exclaimed. Turning quickly, he grabbed Chip's arm. "Chip, go with Phillips. Take one of the taxis outside, pick up the shoes at the Y, and get back here as fast as you can."

Bill Bell had watched the explosive activity in amazement. "What a story!" he said, eyeing Mrs. Phillips. "I understand you were opposed to your son playing basketball."

"That's not entirely true, Mr. Bell. Branch loves basketball and has always wanted to play on a team. But with his job and school and the farm work, he's never had much time, since his father died, that is. He's never complained though.

"And, frankly, I never realized how much basketball *really* meant to him until tonight. You see, he and Chip Hilton have become friends. I think Branch experienced a sense of frustration when he saw Chip forced to play against such a tall player. Sitting here tonight, watching a game for the first time and listening to him cheer for the team, well, I began to appreciate what being on a team and playing for a school could really mean for him."

Branch was shifting awkwardly from one foot to the other. "Mom," he said anxiously, "what about the route? And what about my job at the Y?"

"I'll take care of the route until you get back," Mrs. Phillips said firmly. "The girls can help me. And we'll talk about the job when you get back. I'll call Mr. Ward first thing in the morning."

Mrs. Phillips kissed Branch lightly on the cheek. "You forget about everything and enjoy the trip. The girls and I will be all right."

"You'll have help, Mrs. Phillips," Chip said. "Speed! Call Whitty at Grayson's. Tell him to have Biggie, Red, and

Fireball report at the Phillips farm first thing in the morning for wood duty."

"No, that won't be necessary, Chip," Mrs. Phillips protested.

But it was too late. Speed was already on his way to a lobby phone, and Chip and Branch were right behind him.

The taxi driver made fast time, stopping at the YMCA just long enough for Branch to get his shoes and a few toiletries. Then they sped back to Assembly Hall. When the taxi pulled up in front of the arena, Murph Kelly and the team were just stowing the rest of the equipment and their personal gear in the bottom of the bus for the short drive to University Airport.

Chip introduced Branch to the rest of his teammates as they climbed aboard the bus. They walked down the aisle to join Speed and Soapy in the long back-seat bench. All the players welcomed Branch warmly, and Chip could almost feel the lifting of their spirits.

Dom Di Santis grinned happily. "Now that we've got a big man," he said, "maybe I can play someone my own size and have a chance to look *down* on someone for a change."

The flight was short and uneventful. Most of the players slept, and even Soapy snored through the flight attendants' offers of soft drinks and peanuts. Two hours later, it was a sleepy team that lumbered up the Southern Hotel steps.

Chip and Soapy bought cartons of milk from the hotel shop, said good night to their teammates, and headed up to their room. Chip was especially tired and wanted to be well rested for the Southern game. As he undressed and got into bed, he was thinking ahead to the game the next night. He felt sure Corrigan would start Branch. Coach would try to get him ready for regular play as quickly as possible. Well, he thought happily, now he could relax. State had a big man at last.

The team breakfasted at the Southern Hotel the next morning at ten o'clock; went to the local YMCA for a shooting workout, which Corrigan used chiefly to acquaint

Branch with the State offense; and then went back to the hotel to rest until it was time to leave for the game.

Chip and Soapy were sharing a room on the fourteenth floor, and Di Santis was paired up with Branch next door. Soapy was having a hard time relaxing. He fiddled with his bed lamp, surfed the TV stations, and fluffed and refluffed his pillows. Finally, he ambled over to the window and looked out over the city. "Nice view," he said.

"If you like winter scenes," Chip agreed.

A moment later Soapy peered down at the street. "It's a long way down there. Hey, what floor is this?"

"You know. The fourteenth."

"It can't be! The floor below is the twelfth."

"That's right. What about it?"

"Plenty. Where did the thirteenth go?"

"They just left it out when they numbered the floors."

Soapy solemnly shook his head. "Uh, that's bad. They left it out because it's bad luck. You know something? I'm the thirteenth man on the team. That means I've gotta go."

"Why you?"

"Because I was the twelfth man on the list. Now that Phillips has come out, I'm number thirteen. And thirteen means bad luck."

Chip smiled and shook his head. "I don't think so, Soapy."

"Then how come hotels never have a thirteenth floor?"

"I don't know. I never thought about it."

"I know," Soapy said thoughtfully. "It's because they're afraid people who want to commit suicide will jump out a thirteenth-floor window."

"I don't think that's the reason, Soapy," Chip grinned. "I just figure that some people are superstitious and think it's bad luck to have a room on the thirteenth floor. That's all. It's just silly. It means nothing."

Soapy reflected a moment. "Well," he conceded, "I guess you're right."

The phone rang and Soapy answered it. "Room service,"

he said, winking at Chip. "Sandwiches, refreshments, books, magazines—what's that?

"Oh, Branch . . . wait a sec. This is Soapy." Soapy listened for a moment. "It's Branch," he said. "He wants to see you."

"Sure! Tell him to come on over."

Soapy gave Branch the message, hung up the phone, and opened the door to wait. A few moments later Branch paused in the entrance. "I'm sorry to disturb you, Chip."

It was obvious Branch was embarrassed and uncomfortable. But there was something else, and Chip immediately recognized the symptoms. "Come on in and sit down."

Soapy grasped the doorknob and cleared his throat until he got Chip's attention. Then he winked significantly. "I think I'll go down and get a paper. Be right back."

Chip studied Branch and waited until Soapy closed the door behind him. "You're nervous about the game," he said. "Right?"

Branch nodded.

"You're not the only one. I'm nervous too."

"You are?"

"Sure! I'm always on edge before a game. In fact, I can't think about anything else. Don't worry about it."

"That's not all," Branch said. "What if I'm not good enough? What will the fellows think? And Coach Corrigan—what about *him?*"

"No one expects you to step right in and know everything right away, Branch. Coach and all the guys know you haven't been playing. They won't be expecting much of you at all."

"I sure hope not. Man, right now, I don't think I could run the length of the court. My stomach—"

"Mine too," Chip said reassuringly. "Butterflies! Lots of them!"

"Do you think Coach Corrigan will put me in the game tonight?"

"I sure do! In fact, I think you'll start. You don't need to worry, Branch. Just relax and remember why you're here. We all think you have the potential to play great. Trust what's in your heart, not your stomach. We're all in this together, Branch."

Chip had guessed right. In the locker room, just before the game, Jim Corrigan wrote the names of the Southern players on the white board and chalked in his starting lineup.

"Southern is a run-and-shoot team, men," Corrigan said, turning away from the board. "They've won five in a row and they're cocky. If we play their game, we haven't got a chance.

"Let's try to slow it down and give Phillips a chance to get the feel of the game." He looked at Branch. "Don't be afraid to shoot. You're bigger than Johnston, and if you can get him to foul you three or four times, we'll be in great shape."

Dom Di Santis groaned. "Skinner!" he said. "*Six-seven!* Man, I'm *still* looking up!"

"All right, men," Corrigan encouraged. "Let's go."

The Southern fans applauded them when they ran out on the floor. Then the applause changed to a roar, and Chip knew they were excited because of Branch's height. Chip started the warm-up drill and cut under the basket. As he came back up the sideline next to the bench he saw the Southern coach talking to Corrigan. He stopped at the end of the line of players, which was right in front of the two coaches.

"Where did you get *him?*" the Southern coach asked.

"Who?"

"You know who! The big guy."

"Oh, him," Corrigan said innocently.

"Yes *him!* How come he didn't play in your first three games?"

"Just came out for the team. Yesterday! A walk-on. In fact, he didn't have a uniform until today."

"How long has he been in school?"

"This is his second year at State. He's a junior. He spent his freshman year at Southwestern."

It was Chip's turn to cut for the shot, and he couldn't hear any more of the coaches' exchange. A few minutes later, the players were taking their free throws. Chip had a chance to pat Branch on the back. "Feel better now?"

"No," Branch said miserably. "If anything, I feel worse."

"You'll be all right after the first whistle. Listen! Tap the ball over by the left sideline. Di Santis is giving the signals from his forward position. You know them, don't you?"

Phillips swallowed hard and nodded. "I know them, but I don't think I'll be able to jump."

The referee blew his whistle, and Chip met Skinner, the Southern captain, in the center of the floor. The referee introduced them and briefly discussed the rules. Chip and Skinner shook hands, and then both teams lined up for the start of the game.

Branch stood awkwardly outside the center circle wiping his hands nervously on the back of his shorts.

Then the referee stepped up to the circle and motioned Branch and Johnston to enter. Branch stepped into the circle and crouched awkwardly. But when the referee tossed up the ball, he shot powerfully upward and tapped the ball far to his left. It was a beautiful tap, but Chip had to leap high in the air to catch the ball before it went out of bounds. Soapy's encouraging voice came belting out from the bench: "Atta way, Branch baby!"

Chip recovered his balance, dribbled slowly up to the front court, and waited for Branch to get into position. Then he hit him with a high pass and cut across to set a pick for Jimmy. But Branch stood as if turned to stone. He held the ball high over his head and made no attempt to fake or pass off when Jimmy flashed past. He froze and held his position, tense with stage fright.

"Branch!" Chip called. "Here! Give me the ball!" Branch passed the ball to him as if it were stinging his hands, but Chip flipped it right back. "Shoot!" he yelled.

Branch turned and attempted a hook shot that was way

off line. But Johnston had charged into Branch while attempting to stop the shot. The referee blasted his whistle and pointed to the Southern center for the foul. State's nervous big man walked to the free-throw line with a chance to make the first point of the game.

He bounced the ball several times, obviously trying to postpone the shot as long as possible. Then he swung his long arms upward and released the ball. But the shot was a foot short of the basket, and Southern took the ball out of bounds. The crowd laughed, and several of the Southern fans booed.

Branch's face was fiery red when he dropped back to his defensive position. He looked at Chip and shook his head in despair. Chip picked up Burns, the Southern high scorer, and then checked Branch's defensive position. "Play in front of him, Branch!" he yelled.

Southern's Alpern had the ball, and he waited until Phillips moved in front of Johnston. Alpern then tried to loop it over Branch's head. Chip yelled and darted back to help out. "Up, Branch!" he called. "Up!"

Branch leaped and managed to deflect the ball. Chip grabbed it and started dribbling upcourt. Then he saw Corrigan standing up in front of the bench yelling for a time-out, so he dribbled on up to the ten-second line and called for time.

Coach Corrigan waited until all his players gathered around him. "All right, team," he said. "Nice going." He waited for a second and then reached forward and grasped Branch's arm. He pulled the big player into the center of the circle of players and shook his finger in the pivot man's face.

"Now you listen to me, Phillips," he said strongly. "I'm not taking you out of *this* game or any other game unless you foul out. You're going to start every game and you're going to play every game. *No matter what you do!* That's a promise. Now you get out there and play ball!" He smiled at Branch as the rest of the team joined hands and nodded.

CHAPTER 11

Run-Shoot Game

BRANCH PHILLIPS pressed his lips together hard and squinted his dark eyes when he pivoted out of the huddle and trotted toward the State University basket. Chip grinned to himself. Coach Corrigan knew what he was doing! From now on, Branch wouldn't be worrying about how badly he played. Instead, he would be trying to do his best.

Jimmy inbounded the ball to Chip, who dribbled quickly to the right corner. Then he hit Branch with another high pass and again called, "Shoot!" Branch whirled to his left and banked a right-hand hook shot against the board. It was the same shot he and Chip had practiced so many times in the YMCA gym. The ball whirled lightly against the backboard and went spinning down through the ring for the score.

"Atta way, Branch! Atta way, baby!" Soapy's encouragement floated to the floor from the bench. Chip saw Branch smile with pleasure.

The Statesmen backpedaled quickly, dropping back to stop Southern's fast break. Branch glanced at Chip and grinned happily. And when Johnston took a position just outside the free-throw line and lifted his right arm for a lead pass, Branch's long arm reached out far ahead of the Southern center. His guarding discouraged a pass, and Southern was forced to send another player up for a jump shot. The ball hit the ring and bounced off the backboard.

Chip could have made the rebound, but when he saw that Branch was in position and could get the ball, he pivoted away and sped up the sideline. Branch made the rebound and hit him with a perfect baseball pass far up the court. Chip whipped the ball to Jimmy, who was coming down the center. Tucker was sprinting along the opposite sideline. State had a fast-break going, a three-two situation on Southern's two guards!

Jimmy dribbled to the State free-throw line, faked a shot that drew one of the Southern guards, and then passed to Chip, who had cut along the base line. Chip had an easy shot, but he bounce-passed to Tucker, and J. C. banked the ball in for the two-pointer.

Corrigan had told the Statesmen not to play Southern's game, Chip was thinking, and had warned them about trying to run and shoot with the Southerners. But that was exactly what State was doing, and doing well! There was no reason to change. With Branch using his height and long arms to grab rebounds and then firing the ball to Jimmy, J. C., or himself, State was giving Southern a lesson in run-and-shoot basketball.

At the half, State led by nine points. The score: State 55, Southern 46.

Corrigan was delighted with Branch's playing. When they reached the locker room, he slapped Branch on the back proudly and asked him how he felt. He praised the big man's guarding, rebounding, and outlet passes.

"You're doing great on the defense, Branch," he said. "Great! Your shooting is fine too. But you've been getting away with murder. This half they're going to start to float back to stop your shots. You've got to start passing off to keep them honest. Get it?

"If you don't pass off once in a while, your opponent is *never* forced into a switch situation and he can concentrate entirely on guarding you. Besides that, his teammates can take chances. They can drop off their men and try to tie up the ball. Do you follow me?"

Branch nodded. "Yes, sir."

"Good! Now, if you pass off once in a while and your opponent doesn't switch, your teammates have a chance to get a good unguarded shot. And if you fake to pass and your opponent falls for it and switches off, you have a chance to shoot or drive in to the basket before an opponent can get into position to guard you. Understand?"

Branch nodded again. Corrigan continued, "We have to get going now, but there's one more thing. They will probably change their offense. I don't know whether Johnston can shoot from the outside or not. But I think they'll open up their front court and let him drive. Branch, when Johnston goes outside, play two arms' lengths away from him so we can find out if he can shoot from out there.

"All right, men. Let's keep it up. Oh, yes! It looks as if I was wrong about this team playing the run-shoot game. It looks as if that's right down our alley." He turned to Branch and winked and nodded with approval.

"All right, men. Let's go!"

Taking the inbounded pass, Jimmy brought the ball upcourt. He passed to Tucker, and then the ball went from Tucker to Di Santis and back to Jimmy. Branch had maneuvered into a post position, and Jimmy hooked a high pass in to him. Di Santis cut from the corner, and Jimmy drove right behind the screen and cut for the basket. Then Branch made the mistake of bringing the ball down waist-high to pass off to Jimmy. But the little dribbler's opponent tied him up for a jump ball.

Branch got the tap, but Southern stole the ball. Then the Southerners advanced slowly to their offensive court.

Southern was keeping its front court open and holding two men back to check State's fast break. Johnston moved out to the side of the court. The first time he got the ball, he faked a shot. Branch, fooled, went up with the fake, and the big Southern pivot man drove around him and scored with an easy layup shot.

State came down, and once more the Southern players jammed the middle and swarmed around Branch. They had found the weakness in State's set attack. Branch didn't have enough experience in feeding off the pivot or in ball-handling. The Southerners slowly pulled even and then passed the Statesmen, 76-75.

Corrigan took a time-out and explained what was happening. "You've got to take charge, Chip," he said. "You and Jimmy. Branch hasn't had a chance to learn how to feed off the pivot. Branch, play on the side of the court and leave the middle open for Chip and Jimmy to use some one-on-one stuff."

He laid a hand on Branch's arm. "That means we give the ball to Chip or Jimmy and then clear out. If the passer cuts away from the ball, it opens up the court and they can drive past their guards to score. When they take a shot, you follow in for the rebound."

With Chip and Jimmy employing one-on-one tactics and cutting and driving for scores, State got back in the game and surged ahead 97-96 with three minutes left to play. Southern took a time-out. But it didn't help. In the last three minutes of the game, Chip scored nine consecutive points. Southern could score only three points in the same period of time, and the game ended with State winning 106-99.

The Statesmen hustled happily into the visitors' locker room, yelling, shouting, and pounding one another. They didn't overlook Branch, slapping him on the back, high-fiving him, and shaking his hand. They had a winning team at last!

Chip was looking out the window the next morning when the plane smoothly landed at University Airport. As he walked up the jetway carrying his State University red, white, and blue travel bag, he saw a group of his friends clustered together, waiting just outside the doorway. Biggie, Fireball, Red, Whitty, and Skip Miller were waiting patiently for Chip and the other players to ascend the ramp, and behind them, he could see Mrs. Phillips and three little girls. Chip glanced back at Branch. The big player was marching behind a line of passengers, noticeably on edge and anxious to be back home with his family.

Chip and Soapy followed along behind some of their teammates, and when they reached the concourse, the group enveloped them, welcoming them home and asking questions about the game.

Soapy took over with the game description, and Branch took Chip by the arm and led him toward his mother. "I want you to meet my sisters," he said. He introduced Chip to the three little girls, Jane, Jean, and Joyce, who were eight, nine, and eleven years old, and then kissed his mom.

Mrs. Phillips shook hands with Chip. "Congratulations," she said. "We heard the score last night." She smiled up at her son. "How did Branch play?"

"Great! He played the whole game, Mrs. Phillips."

"And I heard that Chip Hilton got forty-seven points," Mrs. Phillips said kindly. "Gee-Gee Gray said you had scored eighty-eight points in two games. That's wonderful."

"I couldn't have done it without Branch," Chip assured her. "He took care of the boards and Southern's big man, and I didn't have anything to do except score."

"Don't believe *that,* Mom," Branch remonstrated.

Mrs. Phillips shook her head. "Don't worry. Remember, we listened to Gee-Gee Gray. He told us all about the game."

"What did he say about Branch?" Chip asked.

"He said Branch was the best thing to hit State University basketball since Chip Hilton," Joyce Phillips said proudly. She moved close to Branch and grasped his arm.

"What did you do about the deliveries?" Branch asked quietly.

"Do?" Mrs. Phillips repeated. "I didn't do anything! Chip's and Soapy's friends wouldn't let me. I never saw anything like it! They were out at the house before daylight. The fact is, they woke me up with their sawing and cutting. They've got the little shed crammed full of firewood."

"How many showed up?" Chip asked.

"Three. Red Schwartz, Biggie Cohen, and Fireball Finley. If those boys can play football like they can work—"

"You mean *eat!*" Soapy said, joining them.

"They can play football," Chip added.

"But what about the route?" Branch asked. "I thought about it all the time I was gone. Saturday is our big day."

"I was coming to that," Mrs. Phillips said. "After breakfast—" she paused and nodded assuredly toward Chip—"you can be sure I made them eat. Well, about eight o'clock the girls and I got the route book and the truck and started to go into town. But your friends just wouldn't let us do a thing! Biggie drove, I told him where to go, and Red and Fireball made the deliveries."

"What about the girls?"

"Well, Jane sat on the truck with Jean and me, and Joyce went with the boys to make the collections. And you know something?"

She paused and then added triumphantly, "We were through at one o'clock! Oh, and another thing! I called Mr. Ward at the YMCA, and he said you can work around your basketball schedule. He wants to see you."

Branch tried to thank Biggie, Red, and Fireball, but the three of them suddenly found it necessary to head down to the baggage claim to help gather State's equipment and load it on the bus.

Chip and Soapy and the rest of the guys joined the Phillips family for church later that morning. Chip enjoyed the service and the friendly congregation. The Phillipses were active in the church and asked them all to stay for Sunday school. He particularly enjoyed getting to know Branch's young sisters, who were very entertaining.

Then, with several of them in Fireball's Volkswagen and others in the truck, they followed one of the main highways out of University for several miles and turned off on a hard-surfaced road. It was lined with trees and led up a small hill for another mile. They came to a cleared area of about forty acres. A low, rambling one-story farmhouse, framed by a dozen towering pine trees, was backed up against a small rise to the north. A large barn, two smaller buildings, and several woodsheds were located to the right.

Rows of majestic pine trees surrounded the area in every direction, and there wasn't another house in sight. Branch pulled up in front of the house, and everyone piled out of the vehicles. Chip, who had bundled up under blankets in the bed of the truck, had enjoyed the ride. It had been fun, almost like the hayrides he remembered from his Valley Falls High School days.

It was a happy day for everyone. Biggie and Fireball demonstrated their skill with axes and saws, and Soapy and Speed countered by showing their marksmanship with a basketball. Branch had nailed an old hoop on a tree, and Soapy and Speed couldn't miss.

The big event was the midday dinner. There were fried chicken, mashed potatoes, giblets and gravy, homegrown canned vegetables, jellies, preserves, pie, ice cream, and milk. It was a feast for a king.

"Now you understand why we want to kill one another for a chance to come out here and chop wood," Fireball commented.

"You can say that again," Biggie added.

Soapy maneuvered Red and Speed into the kitchen to help with the dishes, despite Mrs. Phillips's protests. Afterward they joined the rest of the guys on four-wheel vehicles for a tour of the farm. Although the majority of the tree farm consisted of pine trees in varying stages of maturity, Branch pointed out different kinds of trees also: white ash, hard and soft maples, basswood, white and red oak, red and white spruce, hemlock, yellow birch, beech, and cherry.

The tour took the group to a pond near the extreme north side of the farm. A hundred feet beyond the pond was a steep cliff entirely bare of trees. The cliff extended three or four hundred yards down to the valley road. It was covered with snow and ice, and the sheer drop forced the guys to edge carefully back from the cliff.

"What a spot for a ski jump!" Soapy said excitedly.

"You mean to commit suicide," Speed retorted.

"Right!" Soapy agreed. "We could call it Soapy Smith's Suicide Ski Slope. Wow! How did I say that?"

After the tour, Branch led them to the woodsheds where the firewood was stored and explained how the bundles were wired. Soapy listened for a while and then sauntered back to the house. He reappeared with a rifle and walked toward the woods. A few minutes later they heard him shooting and walked out to check his marksmanship.

Soapy grinned and pointed to several boards that were leaning against the trees. "Not bad, eh?" he asked. "Take a look."

Speed grunted doubtfully and walked forward to inspect the boards. He leaned closer and shook his head in amazement. "I can't believe it!" he called back. "Look! He hit the center of every circle."

"Five shots and five bull's-eyes," Soapy said nonchalantly. "Well, I guess I'll take a little ride on Blaze. All right, Branch?"

Branch smiled. "Sure. Help yourself."

"C'mon, Speed," Soapy said. "You can ride Thunder."

A few minutes later Soapy and Speed led two draft horses out of the barn, saddled them, climbed on, and rode away through the woods. Branch then showed the guys his power saw and cut a few pieces of lumber. Later, after Soapy and Speed returned from their ride, they all gathered on the big porch and talked basketball and school until the sun sank behind the tree-covered hills. Then Mrs. Phillips and the girls served cold chicken sandwiches, milk, and pie before Branch and Fireball drove them back to University.

Chip and Soapy studied until 10:30 that evening and then got ready for bed. They talked about the Phillips family, the trees, and the food. Just before Soapy turned out the light, Chip referred to the rifle incident. "I didn't know you were such an expert marksman," he remarked casually.

Soapy feigned amazement. "You didn't, huh? There's nothing to it. You see, Chip," he continued glibly, "it's just like shooting a basketball. You fix your eye on the target, aim the rifle just like you aim a ball at the basket, concentrate, and then gently squeeze the trigger. Get it?"

"So far—"

"So far? What else is there?"

"Well, I was thinking there might be an easier way."

"Like what?"

"Well, like shooting at the board first and then drawing circles around the bullet holes."

"Hah!" Soapy said, tightening his lips and glaring at Chip. "You think you're so smart!"

Chip looked at his best pal steadily, with a slight arch in his brow as he studied Soapy.

Soapy stood there a second and then his wide mouth softened, and a grin spread over his face. "Well," he confessed, snapping off the light, "you're right! You're dead right!"

CHAPTER 12

This Was a Team!

BASKETBALL HAD COME ALIVE on the State University campus; it had suddenly jumped into the limelight in the winter sports program. Chip could sense it in the jubilant greetings and happy smiles of his friends and in the basketball talk heard in every building and on every walkway across the beautiful tree-lined campus. Yes, Chip reflected, Branch had put State right back in the national basketball picture. In just one game!

"Believe me! The guy is seven feet tall!"

"They tell me he's the fastest man on the team!"

"I heard he can dunk two balls at the same time! One in each hand!"

"Guess we'll do all right in New York now!"

The team had caught fire too. Chip felt it while he was dressing for practice. His teammates were joking, laughing, and ribbing one another with freedom and enthusiasm. When he walked out on the court a few minutes later, Coach Corrigan was standing near the players' ramp.

"Chip," Corrigan said happily, "come here! Kiddo, you're the greatest! How did you do it?"

"You mean Branch?"

"Of course I mean Branch! Now we can go places. I'm going to change our whole offense, and our defense too!"

Then Chip's teammates caught him up in a rush and carried him with them out on the floor. The Statesmen were red-hot and riding a cloud. They yelled and laughed and applauded each player who made a shot. Their energetic, committed drive as they dashed through the drills brought a wide grin of appreciation to Corrigan's lips. Branch didn't take part in the ribbing, but Chip could see that he was enjoying every bit of the horseplay. The spirit carried on through the long practice session and into the locker room. Even Murph Kelly became infected, loosened up, and managed a few smiles.

Tuesday was rainy and bitterly cold. The wind was a gale that knifed through Chip's sweater and heavy winter jacket as if he were wearing only a basketball net. State's campus seemed almost deserted. Students and faculty members ventured outdoors only when it was absolutely necessary, and even then they scurried quickly from one building to another, shivering from the cold, acting as if they would rather be hibernating like a bear until spring.

But the weather didn't affect the Statesmen's spirits. They were up—way up!—and reported for practice full of dedication and drive. And it lasted right up to the final whistle. Branch Phillips gained confidence with every pass and with every shot. And his defensive play was something beautiful to witness. It was difficult to believe that the addition of one player could so completely change the play and spirit of a team.

That night, when the Statesmen boarded their bus to the airport for their flight to Eastern, the rain had turned to sleet. And the wind was whipping through the trees and streets, driving every living thing to shelter. Kelly didn't have to urge them to board the bus. It was a welcome refuge.

Branch had been the last to arrive at Assembly Hall, and he again joined Chip, Soapy, and Speed in the last seat in the back of the bus. He dropped his carry-on bag on the floor and brushed the sleet from his coat. "I hope Mom gets the truck home all right," he said worriedly, peering out the window to watch the truck disappear into the night. "That road is as slick as glass. I wanted to stay home, but Mom wouldn't stand for it. This storm has me really worried."

"Your mom will make it all right," Soapy said soothingly.

"We'll call her as soon as we reach Eastern," Chip added.

The flight was delayed, and when the team finally arrived at its destination late that night, the weather seemed even worse than it had been in University. The streets were deep with snow and ice and practically deserted. Only the snowplows were moving. Hundreds of cars were stranded, covered over with snow. Fortunately, the airport hotel was only a block away. The players rolled up the cuffs of their trousers and waded through the snow.

The television was on in the hotel lobby, and a reporter was describing the storm and the destruction it was causing all over the country. Chip and Soapy stood in front of the screen watching the weather forecasts, while Andre Gilbert and Murph registered the players and secured their room keys.

Branch went directly to a pay phone to call his mother. He was at the phone a long time, and Chip, Soapy, and Dom Di Santis waited for him. "I can't get through," he said when he returned. "All the lines are down."

They grabbed a burger in the hotel coffee shop and then went to their rooms. Before going to bed, Branch again tried to call home, but he was still unsuccessful in getting through to his mother.

The team slept in the next morning. At ten o'clock the players ate a team brunch together, and then Coach Corrigan held a skull session in one of the hotel banquet rooms before holding an abbreviated practice at the college.

That afternoon, Coach Corrigan took them next door to a movie and then to a pregame dinner. Then he sent them to their rooms to rest. Even there they couldn't escape the storm. There was nothing on the radio or TV except weather news and scenes of the storm.

Branch came into Chip's room and tried again to phone his mom. An operator told him the storm was at its worst around University and that most of the lines were down.

By that evening the road conditions in Eastern had worsened. State University's chartered bus had a difficult time on the icy streets, but the team eventually made it to the Eastern University Field House. At tip-off time, there were fewer than two hundred shivering fans in the stands.

The game turned out to be more of a scrimmage match than an important contest. The nearly empty field house and the absence of the usual crowd noise and cheers seemed to cast a gloomy spell over the Eastern players. But nothing could dull the spirit and enthusiasm of the Statesmen. Starting with the first tap, they took Eastern apart and practically ran them off the court. At the half, State led 61-42. Chip had scored thirty-four points, and Branch had a very respectable fourteen.

Five minutes before the start of the second half, Corrigan asked for their attention. "All right, men," he directed briskly. "Time to go! Line up as you started: Phillips, Di Santis, Chung, Reardon, and Hilton. Keep going, guys!"

Chip easily took the inbound and neatly passed forward to Bitsy Reardon along the sideline. The ball went to Jimmy, over to Dom, back to Bitsy, and then back to Chip. He faked a shot and then hooked a high pass to Branch on the left side of the basket.

Branch faked a return pass to Chip as he cut by and then went up for a twisting jump-push shot that kissed the backboard and went spinning down through the hoop for the first score of the second half. That was only the start. Chip, Jimmy, and Bitsy fed Branch every time they got the ball, and the newcomer kept pouring in the points.

Corrigan cleared his bench and gave everyone a chance, but it didn't stop the slaughter. This was a team! Chip sat on the bench and watched Speed cut and drive with his unbelievable swiftness, and he led the cheers when Soapy took his jumpers. The redhead didn't have to back up from anybody! He could shoot!

The mad pace continued even when Corrigan put in the sophomores. Bill Williams, Rick Hunter, Marty Freedman, and Bo Hicks played like veterans. All the Statesmen seemed to have the touch, right down to the last man on the squad.

When the buzzer ended the game, the Statesmen charged off the court. The team surrounded Chip and Branch, patting them on the back, tousling their hair, and yelling and sweeping them along the corridor and through the door and into the locker room.

"All right! Yes! What a game!"

"What a team!"

"So we were to be Eastern's sixth in a row, huh?"

"Hey, big boy! Hey, Branch! How many did you get?"

"You don't *know?*"

"I know! Twenty-eight!"

"You're kidding!"

"Nope. That's what he got. Plus twenty-four rebounds."

"No!"

"But yes, my fine-feathered friend! And ole dead-eye—"

"You mean me?" Soapy shouted.

"No!" Di Santis exclaimed, grabbing the redhead and pushing him under the shower. "He means Chip."

"I'll bet he got fifty! Hey, Andre, how many did Chip get?"

"Fifty-four."

"You don't mean it!"

Gilbert held the score book up for everyone to have a look. "There it is!" he said jubilantly, pointing to the column. "Right in the book. Fifty-four points!"

"All right, all right, all right," Murph Kelly said, bustling from one player to the next. "Let's get going! Come on, Smith. Fold up that uniform!

"And the rest of you guys, we've got only thirty minutes to get out of here and get to the airport." He turned to the manager and pointed to the door. "You, Gilbert, get out of here and check that bus! Tell the driver we'll be out in five minutes! Do I have to do everything?"

"Hey! Anyone know the final score?"

"You mean you don't know? It was 121-74! We scored three points a minute!"

The Statesmen made it to the airport in Kelly's thirty minutes, but another hour would have made little difference. The computer terminals showed that their flight was delayed. As they watched, they saw the word *Delayed* transform to *Canceled* up and down the screen. The gate crew estimated at least a four- or five-hour delay. The weather in Eastern was bad enough, but the real problem was that flights were grounded just about everywhere else, and their plane was still sitting on the ground in another city.

Branch immediately headed down the concourse to the bank of wall phones, but he came right back. "I still can't get through," he said despondently. Chip and Soapy tried to cheer him up, but it was no use. Branch was apprehensive and worried sick about his mom, sisters, and the trees.

Out of the corner of his eye, Chip saw Coach Corrigan and Murph Kelly, their heads close together, in deep discussion. The small trainer nodded his head and took off rapidly down the concourse to the same bank of phones Branch had just left. Meanwhile, Coach Corrigan went back up to the check-in counter and spoke with the gate attendant, who picked up the phone. Something was up.

Kelly was back in a few minutes and called out, "We're in luck, Coach!"

Coach Corrigan nodded his thanks and smiled. "Men, grab your stuff and meet me down at the baggage claim. There's been a change in plans. We're taking a train. We're going home!"

Eastern's Union Station was located no more than three blocks from State's original hotel. The bus skidded down the snow-covered streets but made it safely. Within thirty minutes, State's weary basketball team was comfortably aboard a warm Amtrak train heading home to University.

A friendly porter assigned the players berths. "I was getting lonesome," he said, smiling broadly. "I'm not used to having a whole car to myself."

Kelly disappeared but was back in a few minutes with the news that he had arranged with the dining-car steward to provide them with a bedtime snack. "Three cars ahead," he said cheerfully. "Sandwiches and milk and all the ice cream you can eat!"

Chip passed up the food and went to bed, but he couldn't sleep. He was worried about Mrs. Phillips and the girls, and it seemed that he tossed and turned for hours before the train finally got underway. He awakened early in the morning and peered out the window at the countryside. Everything was covered with snow: fields, fences, trees, houses, and barns. Few of the roads showed signs of traffic. He dressed and soon found Soapy talking to the porter.

"We're still two hours out of University, Chip. C'mon, let's eat. Murph said he had everything set for us in the dining car. By the way, Coach called off practice this afternoon."

As they sat in the dining car and looked out, it was clearly evident that the brunt of the storm had struck here. And as they neared University, it got worse. Snowdrifts covered roads and fences, and the limbs of hundreds of trees had broken and fallen to the ground. In many cases, whole trees had toppled down. All were heavily laden with ice.

When the train slid slowly to a stop at the station in University, Chip, Soapy, Speed, and Branch were the first to reach the deserted platform. Not a taxi or a car was parked in front of the building. Chip and Branch hurried inside to the phones.

Chip phoned Grayson's right away, and his employer, George Grayson, answered on the first ring. Chip told him about the game and asked if there was any damage at the store.

"We were lucky, Chip," Grayson said. "We're closed except for emergency prescriptions. It's a good thing we had the windows and doors boarded up. We were right in the path of a freak windstorm . . . . No, we're all right."

"Do you need me? I'll be glad—"

"No, Chip. We won't be open for business until Saturday. There isn't a thing you can do. Everything is under control. Thanks for calling though."

Chip rejoined Soapy and Speed, and in a few seconds Branch returned from the phone. "The lines out at the farm are still down," he said worriedly. "I'd better head out for home."

"Wait a minute," Chip said. "Soapy and I will go with you. We don't have to come back until tomorrow afternoon."

"How can we get there?" Soapy asked.

"Walk, I guess—"

"Hold everything!" Soapy said. "I'll check with the stationmaster."

He was gone only a few minutes, but he was bursting with news when he returned. "No taxis!" he sputtered. "No school! No phones out of town! No lights! No water lots of places and no anything! C'mon! We'll walk!"

"How about our suitcases?"

"Don't worry about the bags," Speed said reassuringly. "I'll take care of them."

Hopes for transportation of any kind died as soon as they left the station. The only vehicles in sight were the snow trucks. They were working on the streets, and the three boys found it easier to walk in the trucks' tire tracks than on the sidewalks. Everywhere there was evidence of the severity of the storm.

"Look at the windows," Soapy said.

Many of the windows were boarded up, and the majority of those that were uncovered were cracked and smashed in. Signs were hanging by broken wires and many were down. Snow trucks were working on the main road out of University, and they made fair progress walking.

But when they came to the turnoff, to the asphalt road leading to the farm, there wasn't a tire track, footprint, or even an animal track in sight. The snow was knee-high and up ahead it had drifted as high as their waists. All along the road trees had fallen and blocked the path.

"It must be awful up on the hill," Branch said frantically. "We've gotta hurry."

They managed to make it to the foot of the hill, but then they stopped in dismay. The road was blocked with fallen trees and waist-high snow. And on each side of the road, the force of the wind had tumbled and bent the trees nearly in two. It took two hours of scrambling, climbing, slipping, and crawling to make it up the mile-long hill. They broke into the cleared area and stared with disbelief.

"Look at that!" Soapy gasped.

CHAPTER 13

King of the Forest

GIANT PINE TREES had fallen on the roof of the house. Only the stone chimney remained standing. And all around the cleared area, limbs and branches of trees strewed the ground. The tops of many of the trees had snapped off partway up the main trunk because of the heavy load of ice carried by the limbs. The big barn, the two smaller buildings, and the small woodsheds all looked fine. A wisp of smoke was rising above one of the smaller buildings.

"Thank the Lord," Branch breathed, seeing the smoke. He quickly trudged forward through the deep snow.

There were no trees to contend with now, but the going was still difficult. Some of the drifts were chest-high, and the layer of frozen sleet on top of the snow formed a crust as hard and as sharp as ice. Branch broke a path through the drifts, and Chip and Soapy followed in his footsteps. When they were about halfway to the building, they heard a call and saw Mrs. Phillips and the three girls waving to them. A few minutes later, Branch was hugging his mother, and the girls were telling Chip and Soapy about the storm.

"It was awful," Joyce said. "The wind was blowing so hard—"

"And," Jane, the youngest sister, interjected, "the trees around the house were shaking and cracking like this, CRAAAACK!"

"Mom was afraid they would fall on the house and she said we'd better get out of there," Joyce continued.

"It's a good thing we moved," Jean said. "We got over here just in time."

Branch had been scanning the destruction with somber eyes, shaking his head in dismay. Then he turned toward his mother. "What about the horses, Mom?"

"They're all right, son," Mrs. Phillips said gently. "I put them in the big barn."

Branch turned back and surveyed the tragic scene. "What are we going to do?" he said mournfully. "We'll never get the house fixed up." His voice broke, and he cleared his throat. "I'll get some more firewood," he said, starting for the nearest woodshed.

"I'll go with you," Soapy said quickly.

Chip shook his head and stopped Soapy with his hand. "Let him go alone," he said in a low voice.

Chip and Soapy watched Branch flounder through the snow. Their big friend was a picture of dejection and defeat. His body was bent forward and his head swayed loosely from side to side.

The youngest girl, Jane, stirred restlessly and looked up at Chip. "The trees made a lot of noise when they fell on the house," she said again gravely.

Mrs. Phillips smiled at Chip and Soapy and gathered the three little girls together in front of her like a mother hen with her brood. "It was pretty bad," she agreed, patting Jane on the shoulder. "Now, girls, suppose we get Mr. Chip Hilton and Mr. Soapy Smith inside where it's warm." She gestured toward the building and led the way.

The interior of the building was dimly lit by kerosene

lamps, and at first it was difficult to make out the contents. Then Chip saw that the windows had been covered with blankets and that makeshift beds had been made on the floor in what appeared to have once been horse stalls.

The floor had been swept clean, and there were a table and several benches in the center of the area. The pot-bellied stove caught Chip's eye. Attached to it was a stovepipe that extended out through the side of the building. The sides of the stove were cherry red, and it heated the entire building. Against one wall was a small kerosene cooking stove, and kindling wood was piled high along the opposite wall.

"My husband's parents lived here when they were first married," Mrs. Phillips explained, "before they moved into the homestead. Then it became a horse stable, and about a year ago Branch cleaned it out and made it into a playhouse for the girls."

"Playhouse!" Soapy said, looking around. "It's big enough to be a dormitory."

"It will be *our* dormitory for a long time, I'm afraid," Mrs. Phillips said grimly.

"What's upstairs?" Soapy asked.

"Just a loft. It's full of maple-syrup buckets and the usual odds and ends that accumulate on a farm. However, we'll have to clean it out and make some bedrooms up there."

"It's a good thing Branch fixed it up," Chip said. Mrs. Phillips smiled and nodded. "It certainly is."

"It took nearly all day to move our things," Joyce said.

Mrs. Phillips gasped and clapped her hands together. "Imagine!" she said. "I forgot to ask who won the game."

"We did!" Soapy said. "Chip and Branch killed 'em!"

"Well," Mrs. Phillips said, sighing heavily, "that's something to be thankful for. Let me have your coats. Jean, you call Branch. You boys will be catching pneumonia."

Branch came in with Jean after a few minutes and placed an armload of firewood carefully beside the stove. He turned and attempted a smile. "Well," he said, "we won't have to worry about firewood."

"We never had to worry about that," Mrs. Phillips said softly. "How about taking Chip and Soapy into the old grain room and giving them some of your clothes," Mrs. Phillips suggested. "And you change too."

Branch led the way into the grain room and dug through a pile of his dry clothes. They dressed quickly. And, despite the tragedy of it all, Branch was forced to grin as he gazed at Chip and Soapy. Each had rolled up the jean legs and shirt sleeves but was lost in the oversized garments. Mrs. Phillips smiled when they appeared. The girls tried to hide their amusement, eyeing and nudging one another, but it was hard to do, and they, too, burst into laughter. The incident was a welcome release from the tension gripping all of them.

Mrs. Phillips heated up some soup, and the girls served the boys at the table. Chip and Soapy pitched in hungrily, but it was obvious that Branch had to force his appetite. When they finished, Chip suggested that Mrs. Phillips make a list of things that should be done first.

"The girls and I took care of the horses, the food supplies, and the cooking and eating utensils," she said. "But there are lots of things in the house we couldn't get out. We need the kitchen stove most of all. And beds and dressers and chairs and more towels and sheets and pillowcases."

"No problem!" Soapy said, leaping to his feet. "Let's go!"

Mrs. Phillips and the girls had shoveled a path to the house and the barn, and the boys were soon at work. With his gasoline-powered saw, Branch cut through the trunks of the big pine trees. It was dangerous work, and Chip was glad when it was finished. The logs were too heavy for them to lift, but Branch got some logging chains and pulled them away with the horses. After that, they crawled under the battered roof and into the kitchen and managed to get the big kitchen stove out. That was the big job, but the rest of it was far from easy. When darkness and utter fatigue ended their efforts, Mrs. Phillips's new abode was jammed with familiar furnishings.

The girls had served them sandwiches and hot coffee at different times during the day, but now Mrs. Phillips set the table with steaming bowls of stew, fresh salad, bread and butter, milk, and pie. Soapy proved his eating prowess right then and there, to the delight of the girls and Mrs. Phillips.

They had just finished eating when they heard the heavy and steady roar of motors. "Snow trucks!" Mrs. Phillips said. "I knew they would come. Branch, get a lantern and go out and meet them. I'll make some more coffee."

They hurried to the door and walked outside. Right below the house they could see the lights of the equipment breaking into the clearing. Ten minutes later a huge yellow bulldozer, closely followed by a snowplow, paused on the road near the house.

Branch went to meet them and was soon back with the crew.

"Hi, Mrs. Phillips," the foreman said. "We got here just as soon as we could." He jerked his head back toward the road. "That hill was the worst stretch of road I've seen in thirty years of highway work. If it hadn't been for Fred and his bulldozer, we couldn't have gotten up here for a week."

Later, after the road crewmen had finished their coffee and had gone back to work, Branch lit another lantern and then he and Chip and Soapy went up in the loft and arranged their beds. Soapy was in no mood to talk. He pulled off his shoes, grunted wearily, and climbed between the covers, clothes and all. And he was asleep before Chip and Branch even had time to pull off their woolen socks.

Chip was just drifting off to sleep when Branch whispered, "Chip, are you awake?"

"Yes, Branch."

"I guess you know I'll have to quit basketball." He paused and then continued hesitantly. "I might even have to drop out of school until I can get the house fixed up. Mom and the kids can't live like this."

"How about insurance?"

"We didn't have storm insurance, Chip."

Chip didn't have the heart to say anything more about basketball. It just wasn't the time. But a feeling of dejection welled up in him. Why? Why did this have to happen now? And especially now, just when everything was looking so bright?

Soapy's heavy breathing was the only sound for a long time. Then Chip resumed the conversation. "Can't you sell some lumber?"

Branch sighed deeply. "The good pine's not ready to be cut for lumber, Chip."

"The trees that have been damaged by the storm must be good for something," Chip mused aloud.

"Sure!" Branch said bitterly. "Firewood!"

The sun was bright and warm the next morning, and Branch got the truck going and drove down the hill to the main road for food supplies. Soapy went along, but Chip remained behind. He wanted to have a little time to look over the homestead. A germ of an idea had been building up in his mind all night. If he could get hold of some big jacks and some steel expansion posts, the Phillips family could have a roof-raising party. Besides, Biggie knew a lot about plumbing, and Red's father was in the home construction business.

The truck was back an hour later, and Soapy was yelling before it came to a stop in front of the barn. "Hey, Chip. The game with Northern State has been canceled, and there's no practice until Monday. I called Mitzi and told her about everything and she talked to Mr. Grayson and he said we didn't have to come in to work until Saturday afternoon."

The redhead was out of the truck now and came puffing toward Chip through the snow. "Oh, and Speed and Biggie and Red and Fireball promised to come out Sunday and work all day. Branch is going to pick them up first thing Sunday morning. What do you think about that?"

"I think it's great. Now come on and let's get to work."

Chip and Soapy learned a lot of things that day. While they worked, Branch talked to them about the various trees that grew on the farm and the use to which they could be put. "The most important conifer," he explained, "is the white pine, the kind that fell across the house. It's called the King of the Forest and is used to build almost anything and everything. In the olden days it was used for ship masts."

Later, Branch told them how the trees were cut and logged out of the woods and taken to a sawmill. "After the log is cut and the green boards are ready to be piled, small crosspieces are laid in between to keep them from warping," he lectured.

It was an educational lesson for Chip and Soapy and a release for Branch. It gave him a chance to talk the hurt and despair out of his heart.

Branch drove them into Grayson's Saturday at noon, and Chip and Soapy went immediately to Mr. Grayson's office to thank him for permitting them to stay the extra day at the farm.

"It was nothing," Grayson said kindly. "I don't think we've had fifty customers all morning. Is there anything *I* can do to help the Phillips family?"

"I don't think so, Mr. Grayson," Chip said. "They're pretty proud—"

"They're wonderful," Soapy added.

Grayson's lips softened into a warm smile, and he studied Soapy's earnest blue eyes for a brief moment. Then he nodded in understanding. "And they have two wonderful friends," he concluded.

Business was slow that night at Grayson's, and Chip had time to line up his pals for the Sunday trip to the farm. After arranging for them to meet him at Pete's restaurant the next morning, he and Soapy headed straight for bed. And when Branch drove up to the restaurant after church Sunday morning, everyone was there, waiting in anticipation.

It was a beautiful day, the sun was warm and bright, and it was amazing to see the progress Chip and his friends made in cleaning up the storm's damage at the farm. Mrs. Phillips had her big stove going, and the result was another of her wonderful dinners.

Chip and the guys wanted to keep working, but they had school to think about. Branch drove them back to University, dropping them off in turn at their places of residence. When they reached Jefferson Hall, Soapy, Speed, Biggie, Fireball, and Red told Branch good night. Chip lingered behind.

Branch opened the cab door and stepped down beside Chip on the snow-covered sidewalk. "Chip," he said seriously, "Mom and I want you to know how much we appreciate what you've done for us."

"This isn't good-bye, Branch," Chip said quickly. "The guys are still going to help you with the firewood."

Branch shook his head. "No, it isn't fair. I won't need any help with the firewood, Chip, now that I've dropped out of basketball. You'll tell Coach Corrigan, won't you?"

"I don't want to," Chip said slowly, "but I will. He's going to be awfully disappointed. I still think we can work it out so you can play."

"It isn't right."

"But you don't understand, Branch. We're your friends."

"I know," Branch said slowly. "You and Soapy and the rest of the guys are the kind of people I always dreamed of having as friends. But you aren't responsible for this."

He pivoted swiftly away and climbed back up into the cab of the truck. After a moment he leaned forward and shifted the truck into gear. "Good-bye, Chip," he said brokenly. "Thanks a million for everything."

Just
Could Be!

CHIP STOOD on the sidewalk until the truck had disappeared. Then he went slowly up the walk toward his dorm. The storm had knocked everything down: the Phillips's house, State University's basketball hopes, and all of Branch's dreams. He was deep in thought and didn't see Soapy until the redhead moved out of the shadows. Chip stopped and leaned against a porch pillar. "I guess you know what he said, Soapy?"

"I know," Soapy said bitterly. "Now what?"

They stood quietly in the darkness for several moments. Soapy broke the silence. "I think I'll go get the Sunday papers," he said. "I don't feel much like studying."

Chip nodded but turned away without answering. He walked up to his second-floor room and found his other friends waiting. They were lounging on the beds and chairs.

"He's going to quit the team!" Speed said flatly. "Right?"

Chip nodded. "That's what he said."

"Look, Chip," Biggie said, "all of us have extra time. Why can't we keep on helping him with the firewood route?"

"He says he doesn't need any help, Biggie. He said he was going to quit basketball. I'm just afraid he might quit school too."

"Man, there goes the Invitational," Speed said grimly, getting to his feet. He shifted awkwardly from one foot to the other and continued, "Well, I've got some studying to do. See you in the morning."

One by one, Chip's friends followed Speed's example and left the room. Biggie was the last to leave. He paused at the door. "I know how you feel, Chipper," he said. "I guess we all feel the same way." He closed the door softly behind him.

Chip took his philosophy textbook down from the shelf, sat down at his desk, and tried to study. But, like Soapy, he wasn't in the mood. He stood up and walked over to the window. The branches of the tall elms lining Jeff's sidewalk were stiff and heavy with snow. A moving figure caught his eye, and he saw Soapy scuffing dejectedly along the sidewalk, the papers under his arm.

A moment later the redhead entered the room and slammed the door. "Nothing in the papers but snow and ice and storms and trouble and—well, man, nothing's right. There just isn't any justice!" He handed a paper to Chip, dropped down on his bed, and opened the paper to the sports pages.

Chip glanced at the first page of his paper. Soapy was right. The entire front was covered with stories of the storm. Chip leafed back to the sports section, but before he had a chance to read further, Soapy interrupted him.

"Listen to this! It's Bill Bell's column. Check out the headline: 'State Seen as Emerging National Hoop Power.' That's the headline. 'Seven-footer Provides Big Punch!' That's the line below.

"'Nine days ago the State basketball team seemed headed for a disastrous season. The Statesmen had lost two games before Chip Hilton, an all-American and the country's leading scorer, joined the team. Many fans felt that the presence of Hilton in the lineup would change the picture. But one man doesn't make a team even if he is one of the greatest basketball players of this or any other generation. The big problem was every team's problem . . . height! So, State lost another game—the third in a row. . . .'"

Soapy paused and looked at Chip. "He hasn't seen anything yet!"

He jerked the paper fiercely and continued. "'Then, one Branch Phillips, eighty-four inches of timber-tough bone and muscle, walked in from University's Agriculture and Forestry School and changed the whole picture.

"'State immediately beat Southern 106-99 and Eastern 121-74 for an average of slightly over 113 points per game.'"

Soapy paused and nodded grimly, before reading further. "'Freed up from board and big-man defensive work, Chip Hilton scored forty-seven and fifty-four points, respectively, in the Southern and Eastern games to average more than fifty points a game.

"'So, when Jim Corrigan heads off at the end of this month for his sabbatical immediately after the Madison Square Garden Holiday Invitational Tournament, he will undoubtedly walk off the court with a farewell present of the championship trophy.'

"Oh, sure!" Soapy said bitterly, tossing the paper on his desk. "Oh, sure!"

Chip laid aside his paper and reached for the *Herald*. There was a story about the cancellation of the Northern State game and a list of college scores. He noted idly that Southwestern had won another game and remained undefeated. Then he turned the pages to the classified section.

"What are you looking for?" Soapy demanded.

"The Phillips's firewood ad," Chip said. "Here it is, Soapy."

Soapy looked at the newspaper over Chip's shoulder, and the two friends read the ad.

JUST COULD BE!

Soapy grunted and moved back to his desk. "Humph! Terrible! No pizzazz! Branch really needs some marketing help."

Chip glanced on down the column. There were several firewood ads. Then, suddenly, one ad fairly leaped up at him. He straightened up in his chair and shoved the paper directly under the light. Then, leaving it there, he yanked open his desk drawer and pulled out scissors. Spreading the paper out on his desk, he cut the ad out of the paper and began to read it slowly and carefully.

"Bill Bell's column, eh?" Soapy asked. Without waiting for a reply, he continued, "Bell's a great guy. Best writer in this town for sure. I wonder why no one ever writes a column like that about me?"

He leaned on his elbow and studied Chip curiously. "Hey, you didn't hear a word I said! What gives?"

When Chip made no reply, Soapy leaped to his feet, again leaned over Chip's shoulder, and read the ad.

"Could be!" Soapy said excitedly. "It just could be!"

"I think so too," Chip said eagerly. He ran his forefinger along the lines of the ad and read aloud the kinds of logs wanted. "'Balsam fir, red cedar, red spruce, white spruce, hemlock, hard maple, soft maple—' Soapy, Branch has all those trees on his farm and a lot more!"

He handed the clipping to Soapy and began to unlace his shoes. "I'm going to bed!" he said decisively. "Right now! And I'm going to call on University Wood Products Company first thing in the morning."

"Want me to go along?"

Chip shook his head. "No. I'll do it myself. Besides, if this turns out the way I think it will, I'll need a lot of your help later. Let me have that alarm clock."

Chip set the alarm and then placed the clock under his pillow. He slipped off his clothes and piled into bed dead tired and badly in need of sleep. If everything went all right, Branch and Mrs. Phillips had a surprise coming!

Soapy yawned and glanced at Chip. Then he looked longingly at his bed, breathed a deep sigh, and turned the shade of his study light away from Chip. He reached for one of his psychology textbooks and began to study.

Chip glanced at the wooden sign above the wide gate and walked up the steps to the office. "University Wood Products Company" was painted in the center of the glass door. Down in the left corner was the name "Paddy Clark, President" embossed in gold leaf.

Chip knocked on the door and entered. A low railing formed a small vestibule just inside the door. On the walls were photographs of men and women standing at the edges of rivers and streams, proudly holding rainbow and brown trout. Beyond the entrance way, in the center of the large office, a man dressed in rugged outdoor clothing was sitting at a desk looking over some papers. He glanced up with a quick smile and said, "Can I help you?"

"I hope so," Chip said, smiling in return. He pulled the ad out of his pocket. "Are you Mr. Paddy Clark?"

"I'm Paddy Clark. Say, I recognize you—you're Chip Hilton, aren't you?"

Chip nodded. "Yes, sir."

"Well," Clark said warmly, "this *is* a surprise. I've seen you play basketball, but I've never had a chance to meet you. Come in." He gestured toward a chair beside the desk and extended his hand.

After Chip shook Mr. Clark's hand, he sat down. Clark looked at Chip quizzically and asked, "Now what in the world could I possibly do for a State basketball player?"

Chip handed him the clipping. "I'd like to see the person who can talk to me about this ad."

Clark glanced briefly at the little piece of paper and nodded. "That's easy enough. I can talk to you about logs and stumpage. What's on your mind?"

Chip told him all about Branch and his importance to the team and how the storm had ruined the Phillips farm. As Chip explained the situation, he could see Paddy Clark's interest increasing. But when he told the manufacturer of his hopes to raise enough money to repair the house and help Branch get back in school, he could see the beginnings of doubt creep into his listener's eyes. But Chip continued to the end and then sat back to wait for the answer.

Clark studied the ad for a minute or so, and Chip had time to appraise the man. The manufacturer was about fifty years of age, as tall as Chip, but with shoulders that were much broader. He outweighed Chip by a good thirty or forty pounds. His light hair was touched with gray and seemed to curl every which way. His friendly eyes were as blue as the trout streams in the photographs. Chip realized then that many of the fishing pictures on the wall were of Paddy Clark himself.

Clark laid the clipping on the desk and leaned back in his chair. "I'm quite a basketball fan, Chip," he said with a friendly smile. "In fact, I played high school ball and even played for awhile at State. So I am perhaps more interested in your project than someone else might be.

"However, business is business and I can't let personal sentiment enter into the picture." He smiled wryly. "Especially when a number of stockholders of University Wood Products Company are considerably more interested in dollars than sports."

He paused and studied Chip for a moment. "I happen to know the Phillips place and I know the quality of timber they have out there. But I'm not sure *you* know what you're getting into. There would be a tremendous amount of labor involved in getting the timber out."

"We can get the labor," Chip said quickly.

Clark smiled. "There's another important point. We have a deadline for the material we need: January first."

"I have a deadline too," Chip said ruefully. "We need Branch for the tournament in New York."

"But we're under contract, Hilton. We couldn't risk failure."

"I won't fail," Chip said impulsively. "I'll *guarantee* delivery."

"Not so fast," Clark said, holding up a hand. "The first step is to have a look at the situation. Can you spare a couple of hours?"

"A couple of days if necessary," Chip responded earnestly.

Clark picked up the plant phone and punched some numbers. After a moment he began to talk. "Frank," he said, "I need the small truck. The four-wheel drive. Throw some chains in the back and bring it around front. All right? Good!"

CHAPTER 15

A Vital Project

BRANCH WAS ASTONISHED. He looked from Clark to his mother and then back to Chip. "Do you mean you've been tramping around through the woods for the past two hours?" he said incredulously. "Why, it's only eleven o'clock and it was dark when you left here last night."

"You should know Chip Hilton by this time," Mrs. Phillips said pointedly.

"I guess that's right," Branch admitted.

"What do you think of the idea?"

Branch glanced at his mother and then back to Chip. "Well," he said slowly, "the idea is fine. But—"

"But what?" Chip asked.

"Well, it's just too much. Chip, you and the guys have done enough for us already."

"*We* don't think so," Chip countered, squarely meeting Branch's gaze.

Branch hesitated a moment and then sighed. "Well, it's all right with me, I guess, but it's a pretty big order. Is it all right with you, Mom?"

"That depends," Mrs. Phillips said thoughtfully. She turned to Clark. "Is there enough of the kind of timber you want on the farm to make it worthwhile?" she asked.

Clark nodded. "Plenty. More than enough. In round figures the contract I'm talking about should come to about fifteen thousand dollars."

"Fifteen thousand dollars," Mrs. Phillips echoed. "Goodness!"

Clark smiled. "That's right! The only drawback is the ability of Hilton and your son to get it out in time to meet my deadline. It's going to take a lot of men to get the trees out of the woods. That's going to cost a lot of money. Labor money."

"How many men?" Mrs. Phillips asked.

"At least a dozen men working day and night."

"That's *my* problem!" Chip interrupted.

Clark nodded. "So you said. But that's not all. It's at least a mile down to the road. That's where we would have to load our trucks. Getting the stumpage and logs down to the road would be another problem."

"How about loading your trucks?" Branch asked.

"I'll take care of that. You just get the stuff to the road, and my men and equipment will do the loading."

Mrs. Phillips looked doubtfully at Chip. "It's a big job, Chip Hilton," she said.

"I'll have plenty of help," Chip said confidently.

"And I'll work day and night," Branch said. "Even if I have to quit school."

"You're not quitting school," Mrs. Phillips said sharply. "You started those courses and you're going to finish them."

"Where will you get the labor, Hilton?" Clark asked.

"I'll get it," Chip said. "I've got to get it. This is important to a lot of people."

"I hope you're not overlooking me," Clark said lightly. "Now, I've got several sources of supply," he continued slowly, "and some of them have enough timber available to meet my deadline with little trouble. However, I would rather do business with you and Branch and Mrs. Phillips."

"You mean you're going to give us a chance?" Chip asked eagerly.

Clark smiled. "Let's just say I'm giving you a tryout. That is—" he paused and smiled at Mrs. Phillips—"if Branch's mother is willing to let you try it."

"It's Chip Hilton's idea," Mrs. Phillips said firmly. "If he and his friends want to give it a try and he thinks he can do it, well, I guess it's all right with me."

"Then let's get down to business," Clark said briskly. "This is the twelfth of December. Suppose I give you a week to see what you can do. A week from today will be Monday the nineteenth. I'll come out here that afternoon, and if it looks as if you can make my deadline, I'll give you a contract. How's that?"

"It sounds good to me," Chip said. "How about it, Branch? Mrs. Phillips?"

"It's up to you, Chip," she said firmly, "you and Branch."

Branch nodded, a determined look coming across his face. "We'll take your tryout!"

"Then we're agreed," Clark said, rising. "Thanks for the coffee. Ready, Hilton?"

Clark drove Chip back to University and then to the student union building. "Before you leave, Hilton," he said, "I'll need the names of a couple of references. Now don't get me wrong," he said hastily. "Personally, I know all I need to know about you. But, as I said before, there are the stockholders—"

Chip smiled. "I understand," he said. "Do you know Mr. George Grayson?"

"Of Grayson's? Sure! Who in this town doesn't know George Grayson?"

"Would he be all right for one reference?"

"Sure."

"I guess the other one would have to be Coach Rockwell."

"Perfect. Well, I guess everything is set. By the way, I'll send Branch Phillips a list of the logs and stumpage and the prices. There's one last thing I would like you to know, Chip. Mrs. Phillips's husband was a friend of mine. That's another reason I'm rooting for your project to succeed."

Chip shook hands with Paddy Clark and hurried into the student union. He sat down at the same table in the corner where he and the guys from Valley Falls usually ate lunch, took out a piece of notebook paper, and made a list of the things he had to do.

His first move was to write down the names of those he could count on to help. Branch headed the list. Then came Soapy, Biggie, Speed, Red, Fireball, Whitty, Skip, and Pete. He studied the list and counted the names. His heart sank. Clark had said it would take at least a dozen men working day and night.

For a moment he experienced a deep a sense of discouragement. It was a big undertaking. Then he shook off the feeling and continued writing. "Come on," he told himself. "Get going!"

To Do—RUSH!
1. Notify guys to meet at Pete's tonight
2. Practice (tell Coach Corrigan about Branch and myself)
3. Grayson's (see Mr. Grayson)
4. Set up a stockroom program for Skip
5. Call professors about exams
6. Call Branch
7. Meeting at Pete's
8. Go to bed early

He hustled all that afternoon and evening, working down his list and checking off each item as it was completed. Fortunately, the Phillips's phone line had been repaired, and he arranged for Branch to bring the truck and meet him at Pete's restaurant at 6:30 the next morning. When he went to bed that night, he had completed all his plans for the project.

Soapy was trying to study by the light of his desk lamp, but Chip could hear him stirring restlessly. After a few minutes the redhead pushed his books away and broke the silence. "Chip," he said nervously, "do you really think we can do it?"

"Of course I do, Soapy!"

"What did you say to Coach Corrigan?"

"I told him Branch couldn't practice for a couple of weeks because of the damage to his mother's house."

"What did he say?"

"There wasn't much he could say. But I know he was disappointed."

"Did you tell him what you were trying to do?"

"No."

"Why not?"

"Well, it might not work out. I don't want to build up his hopes."

Soapy thought that over for a moment. "How about practice?"

"I told him I would like to help Branch for a few days."

"How about Speed and me?"

"I didn't say anything about you and Speed."

"But—"

"Now wait a second. All three of us can't stay away from practice. You'll have plenty of time to work. Both of you! There are only four more days of school, and then you can work all day. And," he added grimly, "all night too! Besides, six of us will be enough for the first day."

"Time doesn't wait."

"I know it, Soapy."

"What about the store?"

"Mr. Grayson said I could take as much time as I needed just as long as the stockroom is covered. Skip is going to take care of that. He did say you and Fireball and Whitty could work out a shift with the other employees to take some time off from the fountain."

"Well, that's something," Soapy growled. "Oh, and what about your exams?"

"Already taken care of. I took one today and arranged to do the others as take-homes."

"Well, you'd better get some sleep. I think I'll turn in too."

Chip had set the alarm for six o'clock the next morning and had hoped to slip out without awakening Soapy. But the redhead beat Chip and the clock and hopped out of bed as soon as Chip stirred. "Morning," he said, yawning. "I'm going down to Pete's to see you off."

Chip knew he couldn't win with Soapy, but he tried anyway. "That's silly. There's no reason for doing that, Soapy," he said.

"I know what I'm doing," Soapy said cheerfully.

They dressed quickly and slipped quietly down the stairs and out the front door. Then, despite Soapy's protests, Chip broke into a trot, and they jogged all the way to Pete's restaurant.

As soon as he turned the corner on Tenth Street, Chip saw Branch waiting with the truck. The cab of the truck was filled with people, and the back was loaded down with a lot of others who weren't supposed to be there.

Right behind the truck, he saw Pete Thorpe and Jimmy Chung placing a coffee urn in the restaurant owner's car. "C'mon!" Pete shouted good-naturedly. "You're late!"

"Where are *you* going?" Chip demanded.

"With *you*," Pete said, grinning.

"But what about the restaurant?"

"The day shift can handle it. I'll work tonight. Come on! I'm going!"

"Me too!" Jimmy said. "And look at the truck—we're all going!"

Chip turned and began to count heads. In addition to Branch, Biggie, Red, Fireball, and Whitty—who were supposed to go—Chip counted six more jammed in the truck: Speed, Dom Di Santis, J. C. Tucker, Rudy Slater, and Bitsy Reardon.

"Don't forget me," Soapy said. He vaulted over the side of the truck and landed on top of the protesting group.

"You double-crossed me, Soapy!" Chip yelled in surprise. "You *all* did! What about your exams?"

"We did some rescheduling just like you did!" Dom yelled.

"But what about practice?"

"Pete's going to drive us in," Dom retorted. "C'mon now. Let's get goin'!"

"But what about food?" Chip protested. "Mrs. Phillips can't cook for all of us. There's too many of us."

"She doesn't have to cook!" Pete yelled. "What do you think I've got in the trunk of my car? So just get in and stop arguing. You're riding with me and Jimmy."

CHAPTER 16

Possession Game

"NOW WHAT?" Pete asked, nodding ahead toward the truck. Branch had pulled over to the side of the road and was adjusting the hubs on the front wheels.

"He has to put the truck in four-wheel drive," Chip explained. "That's the only way a car or a truck can get up that hill."

"How about me?" Pete asked. "I don't have four-wheel drive."

"He'll be back for us. Park over on the side of the road."

True to Chip's words, Branch returned in a few minutes, and Pete and Jimmy loaded the food and climbed into the back of the truck. Chip rode in the cab.

"Everything is all set," Branch said. "Mom laid out the job plans last night."

Mrs. Phillips was talking to the rest of the guys in front of the house when Branch parked the truck next to the building. They piled out, and Chip introduced Pete and Jimmy to Mrs. Phillips.

"Food!" Soapy shouted, leaping on the back of the truck. "Give me a hand here!"

Mrs. Phillips invited everyone into the house, and Branch checked their clothing. Some of Chip's friends had come ill prepared for the work, and Branch and his sisters dug out extra boots, stocking caps, and durable work gloves. When they were all suitably dressed, Mrs. Phillips handed the job list to Chip. "You can fill in the names," she said. "Branch will explain the work."

Chip quickly ran through the list and selected who he thought was best suited for the jobs, and they all tramped outside. The sun was rising over the treetops now, and the glitter of the snow and ice on the trees made the scene unbelievably beautiful.

Soapy made the first move. "Well," he said, "I figure you might as well get wet sooner rather then later. Follow me, men!" He ran at full speed and dove headfirst into a high snowdrift below the road. Speed and several others followed behind him, and then they walked along behind Chip and Branch to the barn.

Chip had assigned Soapy and Speed to the draft horses, Blaze and Thunder, and the two friends immediately engaged in a fiery debate, arguing about which horse had the greater racing ability. Branch and Chip gave the other timbermen saws and axes and shovels and chains. The entire troop headed for the jobs with enthusiastic gibes and comments. It was a good beginning.

The first task was to clear the logging trail to the hill road. Other paths would join this main trail. They would then have to haul or tow the logs and stumps to a loading place beside the hill road. It had been fun up to this point. Now it was work! But they pitched in willingly, and when they encountered a log or tree they couldn't handle, Soapy and Speed used the horses to drag it out of the way.

It was a tough job. The snow was deep and the footing was tricky, but spirits remained high and no one complained. After the guys had cleared the main trail, they ranged through the woods in crews and opened up smaller paths leading to the main path. The sun was nearly in the noon position by the time they completed this task. Then Chip and Branch split them up into logging crews.

The work became more fun now. Branch marked the trees and stumps, and the crews trimmed them down with axes and saws. Branch and Chip cut the logs and stumps into the proper lengths with the power saw. Soapy and Speed used the horses and logging chains to drag the wood to the side of the main path. And slowly but surely the pulling and slipping and struggling began to produce evidence of progress.

Soapy, as could be expected, was the first to hear the dinner bell. "Food!" he yelled, clambering up on Blaze. "Food! Let's go!"

Mrs. Phillips, Pete, and the girls served the lunch buffet style. The guys realized they were a lot hungrier than they had thought when they caught their first whiffs of chicken soup, roast beef, and mashed potatoes and gravy—all of which they swallowed down with steaming coffee. They topped off with homemade peach cobbler.

Then they went back to work. At three o'clock the bell rang again, and Branch, Pete, and the basketball players started their trip down the hill and back to town for practice.

To Chip's surprise, Branch was back in a few minutes, and Pete was with him. "What's wrong?" he asked.

"Not a thing," Pete said. "Jimmy drove the car."

"Pete said it would be foolish to drive the truck all the way into town. The whole bunch piled in his car," Branch added.

"Stop gabbing and let's get on with it," Pete said quickly. "I came out here to work off some weight."

They worked until it was too dark to see. Chip was so tired he could hardly walk, and he knew his friends all felt the same way. But none of them would have admitted it.

They walked back to the house and finished another of Mrs. Phillips's wonderful dinners. Afterward, they lounged around the room talking timber and logging operations as if they had been in the business all their lives.

Chip and Branch moved over to a small table in the corner of the room to discuss a daily transportation schedule, and Pete joined them. It worked out that Branch would have to spend too much time on the truck, and Chip was worried about it.

"It's no good, Branch," he said. "We need you with us in the woods. You're the only one who can identify the trees and logs and tell us how to do the job correctly. No, we'll have to figure out something else."

Pete was listening closely. Now he engaged in the conversation. "I've got the answer to that little problem," he said briskly. "Now you guys listen to me. I've got a restaurant truck and a car. Jimmy can drive the truck, and I'll drive the car, and if we can get someone to drive your four-wheel-drive truck, we're in business."

"Mom can drive the truck," Branch said quickly, "But I don't think it's fair to tie up *your* car and truck."

Pete waved Branch's protests aside. "I know what I'm doing. It's good business. If it wasn't for Jimmy and Chip and all the athletes coming around to my place, I'd be out of business. I guess I've got a reason to root for State's basketball team too."

"I think we could get along with just the truck," Chip said.

"Nothin' doin'!" Pete said quickly. "Jimmy and I are in this up to our ears, and we're going to stay in it! Now quit jawing."

That was that. Chip and Branch grinned and called it a day. So the guys tramped out of the house, piled into the truck, and made their way back to University. Branch dropped Chip, Fireball, and Whitty off at Grayson's and continued on to the campus.

Chip hurried into the stockroom, and Fireball and Whitty quickly put on their red and blue polo shirts and white slacks and headed for the fountain. Skip had everything under control in the stockroom, and a few minutes later Soapy came back to tell Chip about practice.

"What a dead workout," the redhead said in disgust. "The guys who worked out at the farm couldn't run as fast as Blaze and Thunder. I'm definitely glad we weren't playing anyone this afternoon. We couldn't have beaten Branch's little sisters!"

"We'll be all right tomorrow night."

"Not without Branch we won't, or at least we won't be the kind of team that's gonna win the Invitational."

"We're doing all we can, Soapy. Keep in mind that we'll have Branch all year if we can finish this thing."

Soapy nodded glumly. "I know. But it would have been nice to win the Invitational for Coach Corrigan."

"We haven't lost it yet," Chip said hopefully. "Did Coach know you guys were out at the farm?"

"I don't think so. I know that none of our guys said anything. How did it go after we left?"

"Fine. Branch said he thought we would make the deadline if we could keep going as we did today."

"Well," Soapy sighed, "that's something. Hey, Chip, don't forget we play Mercer tomorrow night. Coach said we're leaving by bus from the front of Assembly Hall tomorrow afternoon at four o'clock."

The redhead went back to the fountain, and Chip helped Skip fill some orders. The high school star left after nine, and Chip worked alone until ten-thirty. Then he joined Soapy, Fireball, and Whitty and walked down Tenth to Pete's restaurant. Chip made sure Pete was all set for the next morning, and then he and Soapy set out for Jeff and bed.

It was hard to get up Wednesday morning, but he fought back the temptation to sleep just a little longer and forced his tired muscles into action. Soapy was awake, but he played possum. Chip pretended to fall for the fake. He shaved and showered and, sure enough, when he came out of the bathroom, Soapy was fully dressed and waiting.

"Fooled you, huh?"

Chip grinned and took off. Soapy ran after him, and they found Speed, Biggie, Red, Whitty, and Fireball waiting for them downstairs in the hall. A few minutes later they reached Pete's restaurant. The two trucks and the car were parked by the curb and, inside, enjoying Pete's coffee, were the other guys. Chip didn't need to call roll or make a head count. They were all there!

The work went faster that morning. Their muscles were sore, but they knew what to do about that! All athletes do! The best cure is to jump in and work. So they pitched in and worked without a break until noon. After lunch they worked right up to three o'clock. Then Pete and Jimmy drove Chip, Soapy, Speed, J. C., Rudy, Dom, and Bitsy to Assembly Hall. Jimmy parked the truck, and Pete started back to the farm. The four sophomores—Williams, Hunter, Freedman, and Hicks—were already there at Assembly Hill, and when the bus started for Mercer, State's varsity was complete with the exception of Branch Phillips.

It was a pleasant ride. The roads had been cleared, and it was warm and comfortable in the bus. Usually there would have been a lot of kidding and laughing. But Chip and the timber gang were tired and tried to sleep instead. They stopped for a pregame snack at 5:30 and continued on to arrive at the Mercer Field House right on schedule.

Chip had been thinking ahead to the game and worrying about Mercer's height. And the first thing he did that night when he led the Statesmen out on the Mercer court was to check the home team for exceptionally tall players. There were none, and he breathed a sigh of relief.

Corrigan started a team consisting of Chip, Di Santis, Chung, Reardon, and Speed. It was a fast and fighting team.

The lineup was closely matched in height with the opponents, and the result was an evenly matched contest.

The home team's tactics were quickly evident. The Mercer center got the tap, and his backcourt teammates advanced the ball slowly into the front court. Then they passed and cut, passed and cut, and passed and cut until a teammate could break free close to the basket for a shot. It was the old, monotonous possession game. Chip hoped his teammates would not become impatient and make too many mistakes.

Mercer scored first, and when the Statesmen got the ball, they took off at full speed. But the home team's controlled offense enabled them to maintain good defensive balance, and the Statesmen found it impossible to develop a fast-break situation. So State was forced to go into a set formation. After several passes, Chip set a pick for Bitsy, and the speedster scored with a jumper.

The lead shifted time after time. Mercer would forge ahead, and then State would catch up and pass the home team by five.

At the half, Mercer led by a low score, 34-31. Chip had taken only eight shots during the half, but he had hit on six of them and had scored twice from the free-throw line for a total of fourteen points.

The second half opened with Mercer sticking with its control game. And when the Statesmen couldn't get their fast-break game going, Corrigan called a time-out and substituted Slater for Reardon and Tucker for Morris. Now they had a typical cat-and-mouse contest going with cautious passing and maneuvering until an almost sure shot was possible. Mercer was keeping its under-basket area open and using a cutting game designed to free a player under the basket.

State countered by collapsing in front of the basket. On the offense, the Statesmen concentrated on outside shooting. Chip hit time after time just beyond the free-throw circle, and State went ahead, 59-58, with three minutes to play. The lead forced Mercer to try a full-court press. Corrigan immediately sent Morris and Reardon back into the game.

Now the contest became a hard-running, wild-passing, free-scoring affair. But State managed to stay out in front and the game ended with the Statesmen leading by a single point. The final score: State 68, Mercer 67. Chip had scored thirty-four points.

The team stopped for something to eat on the way back. Usually the players would have been jubilant, happy, hungry, and lighthearted after a victory.

But the spirit was missing. The veterans were done in, completely worn out, not only because of the work at the farm but also because of the close game. Unused muscles were tight and sore, and several of the players remained on the bus, preferring to rest. Those who left the bus ate their food slowly and quietly. All of them knew that Mercer should have been a pushover team; State should have won by twenty points.

Soapy was the first person out of the bus, so Chip walked along beside Coach Corrigan to the restaurant. They ordered sandwiches and milk and shared a small table near the door. After they sat down, the conversation centered around the game and then shifted, as Chip expected, to Branch Phillips.

"To say that we miss Phillips would be the understatement of the century," Corrigan said, smiling whimsically. "Do you think we'll ever get him back?"

"I don't know, Coach. We're sure trying!"

"We?"

Chip flushed. "Yes, sir. Some of the guys have been helping out."

"That's what I figured," Corrigan said carefully. "I hope you're not overdoing it."

The Craziest Thing

TRAINER MURPH KELLY was trembling with anger. His face was red and his eyes were smoldering. He dropped Chip's hands and moved to a position in front of Soapy. "Let's see 'em," he demanded harshly.

Soapy extended his hands, palms down. The little trainer glared angrily at the redhead for a second. Then he grabbed Soapy's wrists and twisted his hands upward until he could see the tender, blister-covered palms. He examined them thoroughly and then pushed them back.

Stopping before each player, he examined his hands and then moved on to the next. Then he walked back to the center of the room. "What's this all about?" he demanded, his voice trembling with emotion. "What have you guys been doing?"

Glaring at each of them in turn, he waited impatiently. But no one spoke. He resumed his raging. "No wonder you've been fumbling all over the place," he exclaimed. "Those hands look as if you've been in a fire. Now what's the answer?" He looked along the line of players.

Not a player said a word. Not a player moved.

"All right!" he rasped. "I know how to get the answer." He turned and stormed out of the training room, slamming the door angrily behind him.

"No emotional control," Soapy observed lightly.

Speed snorted. "Listen to who's talking."

"He's gone to get Corrigan," Dom said.

The players waited silently as Chip thought back over the past three days. It didn't seem possible that this could already be Saturday night and that State would be tangling with Poly-Tech on the local rival's court in another half-hour or so.

The timber gang had almost torn the hill apart. The guys had worked from early morning to dark on Thursday and Friday. Just three hours ago, when Chip and his basketball teammates left to get ready for the game, the football squad had carried on. And what a squad it was! Christmas vacation had started yesterday at noon, and this morning Biggie had shown up at Pete's with nine football players who lived in University.

The whole thing had been a well-kept secret, so far. But now the team was in for it. When an athlete concealed an injury from Murph Kelly, he was in the doghouse. Big time! Permanently!

His thoughts shifted to Pete. If there ever was a champion, it was the popular restaurant proprietor. Pete had carted food out to the farm by the truckload. There would never be a way to repay him.

The door opened, and a still angry Murph Kelly was back. Coach Corrigan followed. "A basketball player is only as good as his hands, Coach," Kelly was saying. "Take a look at these guys!"

"I think I know," Jim Corrigan said, leaning against the table. "Let's see, Chip."

Chip held out his hands, revealing reddened calluses and broken blisters.

"The rest of them are the same," Kelly said angrily.

"I know, Murph," Corrigan said softly. "I suspected this might happen when Chip told me about helping Phillips. I gave Chip permission to miss the practices, you know."

"How about the rest of them?" Kelly demanded aggressively. "*They* didn't have permission, did they?"

"They didn't miss any practices, Murph."

"How about their hands?" the tenacious trainer demanded.

"I have no control over their free time, Murph."

"How about school? You've got something to say about that, haven't you?"

"Not as long as they maintain their eligibility. Frankly, Murph, I feel a little ashamed that *I* didn't offer to help."

Kelly twisted his head to one side and stared at Corrigan incredulously. Then he shook his head. "Well, if this isn't the craziest thing I've ever heard of!" he gasped. "You mean you're going to stand for them reporting with hands like that?"

"I don't like it any better than you do, Murph. But there isn't anything I can do about it. Right now I'm interested only in fixing up those hands and beating Tech."

"You mean that's all there is to it?"

"That's right!"

Kelly stared at Corrigan for a long moment and then turned away. He fumbled with his first-aid kit and produced some gauze and antibiotic cream. "This is about all I can do now," he said gruffly. "If you boys had given me a chance when you first got those blisters."

"Forget it, Murph," Corrigan said sharply.

Five minutes later the Statesmen trotted out on the Poly-Tech floor, and the Tech cheerleaders led a cheer for them. Like most intracity competitions, the rivalry between State and Poly-Tech was keen and spirited. Tech was a much smaller school and could compete with State in only a few sports. But basketball was one of them, and the games were always close and hard fought.

Following the warm-up period, the referee blew his whistle, and he and his assistant walked out to the center of the floor. Chip and the Tech captain joined the two officials for the introductions and a brief discussion of the rules. Then Chip walked back to the State bench where Corrigan waited with the rest of the team.

"Yea Tech! Yea Tech! Fight!"

Corrigan had named Chip, Dom, Speed, Jimmy, and Bitsy as the starting five, and while they waited for the buzzer, Chip thought back to the previous year when Tech had lost only one game. Tech hadn't been on the State schedule, but Chip and Soapy had been friendly with three seniors on the team. He glanced at the Tech players surrounding the home team's bench, but he knew none of them. And when the teams lined up for the center tap, Chip was quick to note that Tech had started a small team.

The game turned out to be a duplicate of the one with Mercer. The Tech starters were three sophomores and two juniors, and it didn't take them long to find out they couldn't match State's speed and experience. Three minutes later the Tech coach took a time-out, and when his players trotted back to resume the game, it was clear he had instructed them to play control ball.

Corrigan watched them play for two minutes and then called for a time-out and sent Tucker and Slater in to replace Speed and Bitsy.

It was a hotly contested game, but State got out in front in the first minute of play and never lost its lead. Tech fought for every point, but the Statesmen were schooled in tight play and managed to maintain the lead and last it out. The final score: State 54, Poly-Tech 52.

Chip had played the entire forty minutes and could scarcely walk off the floor. Tech had double-teamed him all through the game, and he had countered by passing off to feed Jimmy and Dom for easy scores. Even without shooting much, he had made twenty-one rebounds. And despite the Tech defensive strategy, he had tallied twenty-eight points.

After the players showered and dressed, Corrigan kept them in the locker room for a short talk. "We were lucky tonight, men," he said. "Real lucky. Fortunately, that was the last game before the tournament. Anyway, I'm calling off practice until Friday. A little rest will do all of us some good. Now, before you leave, let Murph fix up those hands.

"And, Murph, see that they get something to eat. I guess the best place would be Pete's restaurant." He paused and then added pointedly, "I hear you can find the whole bunch of them there every morning around six o'clock. Well, good night, everyone."

"Now what did he mean by that?" Soapy demanded.

Kelly grunted. "Huh! You think you're slick? Corrigan knows every move you guys make."

The trainer grumbled and griped as he took care of their hands, but Chip noticed he was also gentle and patient. Kelly was still grumbling when he led the way to the bus. Chip and the rest of the players followed along, and Andre Gilbert and the four sophomores fell in beside him.

"We'd like to help," Gilbert said. "We all live here in University."

"Right!" Hunter added. "Count us in."

"Meet me tomorrow morning after church at Pete's restaurant," Chip said, grinning. "And come dressed to work!"

"We'll be there!" Freedman and Williams chorused.

"You're on!" Hicks added.

Chip, Soapy, Speed, Red, Fireball, Biggie, and Whitty hurried to the restaurant Sunday morning after church services. There they found Branch, Pete, Jimmy, Skip, Andre, Williams, Hunter, Freedman, Hicks, Biggie's football teammates, and several new guys Chip didn't know.

"We brought some friends along," Hunter explained. "They want to help."

"Good!" Chip said. "We could use a *hundred* more."

It looked like an invasion when they unloaded at the farm. Chip and Branch placed Biggie, Fireball, and Red in charge of the new crews and furnished them with equipment. Soapy and Speed harnessed the horses and led them out of the barn.

Mrs. Phillips had watched the proceedings in amazement. Now she approached Chip and Branch and grasped each by an arm. "There's never been anything like this on the hill," she said in wonderment. "You certainly have the boys organized. A person might think you've been doing this all your lives."

Soapy led Blaze close to where Chip and Branch stood. "They learn pretty fast, Mrs. Phillips," he said blandly.

"*They* learn fast!" Speed exploded.

Soapy looked at Speed and nodded. "That's right, Speed," he said gravely. "Now, Mrs. Phillips, if you've got the time to walk over to the main trail, I'd like to show you something else I've worked out."

"*Listen* to this guy," Red said. "He's never worked out anything in his *life!*"

Soapy ignored Red's outburst. "If you will follow me, please," he said courteously.

Chip smiled and nodded to the gang and Mrs. Phillips. The entire group fell in line behind Soapy and Blaze. When they had nearly reached the end of the main trail, Soapy stopped his horse and told Speed to hitch Thunder to the empty sled and wait.

"And when Blaze arrives with his load of logs," he said lightly, "send Thunder along, and you and your gang can unload Blaze's load. Then when Thunder gets back with a load, start Blaze back."

"Aren't you coming back with Blaze?" Speed demanded.

"Of course not!" Soapy said indignantly. "He's coming by himself."

"It won't work!" Speed said flatly.

Soapy eyed him disdainfully. "Just do as you're told, my merry man," he said. He waved to his crew. "Shall we proceed, gentlemen?"

Soapy rode Blaze slowly away amid his buddies' playful gibes and jeers, and after a brief moment of indecision, his crew plowed through the snow behind him. Branch, Mrs. Phillips, and the newcomers watched the scene with quiet amusement.

"Speed!" Soapy yelled back over his shoulder. "Hitch Thunder to that sled."

Speed got Thunder ready and sat down on the sled. "Might as well take it easy," he said, yawning. "We'll be here a long time."

But Speed was dead wrong. In less than five minutes, Blaze came plodding along the path, all by himself, pulling a sled piled with logs.

"Man! Who woulda believed it?" Speed managed. He led Thunder and his empty sled carefully around Blaze and turned him loose. Without the slightest hesitation, Thunder put his head down and took off, straight along the trail.

"I can't believe it," Speed moaned. "All those miles we walked leading those two animals—"

"You'll never hear the last of *this*," Red roared.

Mrs. Phillips laughed and returned to the house. The workers all started their assigned tasks. The sun soon reached down through the woods, warming the air and the hard workers, and they stripped off their coats. After a hearty lunch, they dug into the job again. It was still warm, but the sky was clouding over and a light breeze was springing up from the south. And by four o'clock, when Pete came out with hot coffee and sandwiches, the sky had darkened and there was every indication of rain. They worked on until dark, and then Branch, Pete, and Jimmy drove the whole crowd back to University, dropping them off at their respective destinations.

Branch had the guys who lived in Jeff on his truck, and when Chip and his dorm friends piled out, Phillips couldn't conceal his elation. "We've got most of the timber ready," he said happily. "The only thing we have to worry about now is hauling it down the hill. It looks as if we're going to make it."

"And if we do . . . ." Soapy said suggestively.

Branch laughed. "I'll be back in a State basketball uniform."

But Branch had spoken too soon. That night there was heavy rain that froze as it fell. By six o'clock the next morning, it was bitterly cold, and the streets and sidewalks were a glare of dangerous black ice. Chip and his pals could scarcely stand up on the slippery sidewalks. They took to the street, and it was seven o'clock before they reached the restaurant. But late as they were, they were the first to arrive.

Pete and Jimmy arrived soon afterward, driving slowly and gingerly along the icy streets. Chip and the guys were stamping their feet and rubbing their hands to keep warm, and as soon as Pete unlocked the door to the restaurant, they rushed inside to get out of the cold. Then they lined up by the windows to watch for the others. The rest of the timber crew arrived by twos and threes until everyone was accounted for except Branch.

It was 8:30 before he appeared. There were chains on all four wheels of the truck and even then it slid to a stop when he applied the brakes. Seconds later he joined them inside, dejected and beaten. "I can't believe it. The hill is completely covered with ice," he said hopelessly. "You can't stand up! I fell three times just getting to the barn."

"But Paddy Clark is supposed to come today," Soapy said.

"No one can get *up* the hill," Branch said, "which means it will be virtually impossible to haul anything *down* it for three or four days. That means we can't possibly meet the deadline. We did all that work for nothing."

"Oh, no!" Chip said sharply. "Wait a minute! We're not quitting now!"

"But what can we do?" Branch asked.

"Plenty! The ice can be a break for us. If Clark can't get up the hill—"

"He can't see what we've done and he can't say no!" Soapy exclaimed. "Say, isn't there some kind of saying about it being an ill wind that doesn't blow somebody some good?"

"There sure is," Chip agreed grimly.

"We'll never make the deadline now," Branch said gloomily.

"Nothing doing!" Chip said stubbornly. "Don't give up so easily, Branch. We're going to keep right on working."

"But the trucks can't make the hill, Chip," Branch warned. "And you'll never make it on foot. The road is a glare of ice."

"I can whip that," Chip said confidently.

"I know!" Soapy said. "We'll get a rope and hang onto it like people do when they climb up a ski slope. I'll be the leader."

Chip pivoted around and looked at Soapy for a split second. Then he snatched the redhead's cap off his head and sailed it over the counter. "Come on!" he said, grabbing Branch and pulling him toward the door. "Come on, big boy! Our troubles are over!"

CHAPTER 18

Joining Together

"I DON'T UNDERSTAND," Branch protested. "What are you going to do?"

"First," Chip said, pausing at the door, "were going to get basketball shoes."

"Basketball shoes?"

"That's right."

Soapy's yelp startled them. "I get it! I get it!" he yelled. "Remember in football when we had on sneakers and the field was iced over and slippery and we couldn't run? Right, Chip?"

Chip nodded. "Right! Now listen, first we get the sneakers and then we drive out to the farm. All right with you, Pete, Jimmy?"

"Absolutely. We're in. Right, Jimmy?" Pete asked.

"Absolutely," Jimmy echoed.

"But even if we get up the hill, it won't do us any good," Branch said. "Our big problem is getting the logs and stumps we've cut *down* the hill."

"We're not going up the hill," Chip explained. "We're going to build a run-out."

"A what?"

"Hold everything!" Soapy roared. "I know! I ought to know. We're going to fix a track for the Soapy Smith Suicide Ski Slope. Right, Chip?"

"That's right."

"I knew it!" Soapy gloated. "And then," he paused dramatically, "and then we're gonna give all those little ole logs and stumps a ski ride down to the road."

Branch's eyes widened and he turned and looked at Chip in utter admiration. Then a big smile lit up his face. "That's it!" he said excitedly. "Chip, you've done it. It'll work! I just know it will! That slope is covered with a lot of ice and I can keep it covered. I'll run a hose into the pond and pump water over it every night."

"It's an ill wind," Soapy said philosophically.

Branch was nodding happily. "It will save us days and days of hauling down the hill road, and the logs and stumps will end up in the meadow right beside the valley road. Why didn't *I* think of that?"

"Just a matter of brains," Soapy said smugly, trying to reach around and pat himself on the back.

It took them two hours to get to Assembly Hall and find Murph Kelly. It took another half-hour to talk him into letting them have sneakers. And it was another hour before they reached the hill road, but they made it!

A quick glance was all that was necessary to understand why Branch had said it would be impossible to navigate the road. It was covered with thick ice as far as they could see.

Branch, Soapy, Speed, Bitsy, Red, and Marty Freedman were elected to hike up the hill for tools. "You can slide them over the cliff, Branch," Chip said. "And," he added, "we'll need some good-sized logs for a barricade. Don't forget chains."

The climbers put on their sneakers, and Chip watched them until the red, white, and blue tassel on Soapy's red toboggan hat was out of sight. Then Chip and his crew continued along the road until they were opposite the cliff.

Their sneakers worked fine on the ice-topped snow, and they walked across the meadow to the bottom of the steep hill.

"This is great!" Biggie exulted. "There's plenty of room for the timber."

"Now what?" Pete asked.

"We need a breaker so the logs won't slide out on the road and block traffic," Chip said. "We'll use some logs and snow and ice for a base."

"Let's get out of here before we get hit in the head with a shovel or something," Fireball said, looking anxiously up at the cliff.

Half an hour later they heard a yell and saw Branch and his crew standing at the top of the cliff motioning them out of the way. In a few more minutes shovels, picks, crowbars, and chains came sliding and slithering down the slope. Many of them overshot the meadow and slid clear across to the road, but all of them got down the slope cleanly.

Chip's crew gathered them up and barely had time to get out of the way before the logs began to come. They came flying down the slope, turning and rolling and sliding just as the tools had done. When they had enough logs for the breaker, Chip signaled to Branch to stop dropping logs, and they got to work.

They finally finished the barricade at noon. Pete went back to the truck and returned with some soup and sandwiches, which they gratefully accepted. Then it was back to work. The logs and stumps were coming down regularly now, and the guys were kept busy all afternoon pulling them away from the slope and lifting them into piles.

Pete had brought only enough food for lunch, but they kept going until dark. Then, dog-tired and hungry, they climbed aboard the truck, and Jimmy drove back to the bottom of the hill. Branch's crew joined them a little later. Soapy and Speed were arguing about which of them had hauled the most logs. Chip interrupted their argument long enough to learn that Branch was satisfied with the crews' progress.

The road crews had gotten the highways sanded by the next morning, and the going was much better. It was still impossible to get a truck up the hill road, so Branch and the hill crew had to walk again. Chip and Branch had the cliff plan worked out to the last detail. Branch and his crew would assemble a big pile of logs at the top of the cliff. Then, when there were enough, he would signal Chip to get his guys out of the way, and the logs would come flying down. By the time Chip's crew had the area cleared, Branch would have another pile ready. It was a good system.

The county highway crew cleared the valley road early Wednesday morning, and Chip and his gang had been at work only an hour or so when Paddy Clark drove his truck into the meadow. He dropped down out of the cab, looked around at the piles of logs and stumps, and whistled in surprise. Then he walked over to Chip and extended his hand. "Well," he said, "it looks as if I underestimated you young college men. Whose idea was this?"

"It just happened," Chip said, smiling. "How do the logs look?" he asked anxiously. "All right?"

"Fine!" Clark said heartily.

"Good! I was afraid they might be cracked up or something coming down the slide," Chip explained.

Clark smiled. "We wouldn't want them if they were that brittle. No, they look all right. In fact, everything looks so good that I'm going to send my loader and trucks out here right away." He paused and smiled. "That is, if it's all right with you."

"It's all right with me!" Chip said happily.

"Oh, and Chip," Clark said, grinning, "I'll be back Saturday afternoon. If you keep going as you have, you'll have that contract."

Chip's heart leaped. "You mean it?"

Clark nodded. "I mean it. Well, I've got work to do. See you Saturday."

Chip thanked him and turned away, scarcely able to keep from yelling and jumping. They had something concrete to go on at last!

Just as Paddy Clark drove out of the meadow, another car turned in and parked. Coach Corrigan, riding in the driver's seat, tooted the horn, and Coach Henry Rockwell's large hand waved a hello. In the back were Murph Kelly; Dad Young, State's director of athletics; and Jim Sullivan, one of State's assistant football coaches. Chip hurried over to meet them. Corrigan got out of the car and waved a hand at the scene. "It looks as if you men have been doing great things," he said.

"We sure have!" Chip said. "And if we keep moving at the same rate for three more days, I think Branch Phillips will be back in uniform."

"You mean that?" Corrigan demanded incredulously.

"I sure do."

"Well, now," Dad Young said, joining them. "Maybe we can scare up some more help." He elbowed Sullivan, who was close behind him. "What do you think, Jim? Some of your football kids live here in town, don't they?"

"They sure do!" Sullivan said. "Where do they report? What time?"

"Six-thirty at Pete's restaurant," Chip said.

"You can count on them. Me too!"

"And me," Corrigan said.

"I guess the guys in my department can do something," Murph Kelly commented.

It was a strange assembly that gathered at Pete Thorpe's restaurant Thursday morning. There were coaches and trainers and almost two teams of football players, in addition to the regulars who had been on the job from the beginning. Branch was shocked into silence at the sight of Coach Corrigan, Jim Sullivan, Murph Kelly, and his assistants.

But he finally found his voice and told Chip the good news. "Our road is open! They cleared it last night. Any kind of car can make it now. With chains, of course."

That was a big day. Clark's loader and trucks had worked sporadically the previous afternoon, but now they were operating steadily. Friday was the same. The big lumber trucks had difficulty keeping up with the large supply of logs and stumps.

The spirit of this great venture had gripped all of the workers, and Corrigan, Sullivan, and Kelly were no exception. They got right into the thick of it, trimming branches from the logs, loading pallets, and helping to tumble logs over the cliff. The work was moving so well that Coach Corrigan called off practice. "This gets in the blood," he said, grinning. "I think I'm a born timberman. Now I know why the fans keep hollering for a new coach. I've been in the wrong field!"

Clark didn't show up until late Saturday afternoon. Then he called Chip aside and told him that he had been up on the hill and had advised Branch not to trim any more logs or stumps. "All you fellows have to do now," he added, "is get the stuff you've got cut down over the slide and stacked up in the meadow."

"Then we're in!" Chip said excitedly.

Clark nodded. "Just about! Oh, by the way, Hilton," Paddy Clark's blue eyes twinkled, "I gave Phillips a contract. He wants to keep it a secret until tomorrow at dinner. We haven't told anyone else, and we're counting on you to keep it confidential."

"Don't worry, sir."

"Good! I'll be up on the hill for dinner tomorrow afternoon. Branch said it would be ready at two o'clock. Imagine! Christmas dinner for a bunch of hungry athletes in a barn . . . and with only a wood stove for the cooking!"

"Mrs. Phillips and Pete Thorpe are pretty special in the kitchen; it seems as if they can perform miracles!" Chip said.

"What about church and family gatherings?"

"Most of us are going to midnight services. Besides, we're not coming out here until noon. We wouldn't miss tomorrow's celebration for anything."

"I'll sure be here!" Clark concluded.

Christmas morning dawned cold and crystal clear. Chip called his mom in Valley Falls, and they spent nearly an hour chatting away. He filled her in on the progress of the big timber project. It wasn't the first time he had been away from her at Christmas, but both times it had been to reach out to someone in need. Chip and his mom both felt that helping someone else was a blessed way to spend the holiday. Still, they both looked forward to his arrival home after the tournament.

Though Chip and Soapy had gone to midnight services, they returned to church the next morning to sing in the choir. Chip felt there was no better time to sing than Christmas Day. He silently gave thanks for the special miracle he and his friends had put together the past two weeks—it was wonderful to be able to help those in need.

Later, when the timber gang checked in at the restaurant, there were few absentees. Coach Corrigan and several of the players had driven their family cars, so there was more than enough transportation. Pete, Jimmy, and Branch loaded the trucks with food and decorations.

Soapy went behind the lunch counter and produced several large cardboard boxes. "Handle these carefully," he cautioned, handing them to Speed and Red.

It was a happy crew that arrived at the Phillips farm. Chip and Branch had said nothing about the job being completed, but all of the members of the crew somehow seemed to sense it. They drifted away in groups to the barns and across the hill road to the woods, the pond, and the cliff. All were anticipating Mrs. Phillips's Christmas Day dinner.

Paddy Clark drove up the hill shortly before two o'clock with three guests: Bill Bell, sports editor of the *Herald;* Jim Locke of the *News;* and a photographer. And right after Paddy Clark introduced them to Mrs. Phillips, she told the girls to ring the bell. Everybody had been waiting for that welcome sound and came whooping in, laughing and kidding and hungry. They cleaned up under the pump by the homestead and then gathered in front of the barn.

"Where's Soapy?" Speed asked suspiciously.

"Sneaking off as usual," Red said.

"He's around," Chip said mysteriously.

Pete appeared at the door of the barn just then. "All right, everyone!" he yelled. "Come and get it!"

Chip ushered the sportswriters and photographer inside and waited until the coaches and Paddy Clark entered. Then he waved everyone inside and followed, right into a miracle!

Fresh-scented evergreen boughs, mistletoe, and holly hung from the rafters in great sweeping branches. Two long tables covered in bright red and green Christmas linens extended from one end of the building to the other. And a huge live Christmas tree, shimmering and sparkling with festive lights against silver icicles, dominated one corner of the barn. Beside the tree, holding a number of boxes, stood a jolly, chubby Santa Claus. All were amazed by the transformation in the place and stood quietly opposite their places at the table while the photographer took a number of pictures.

Chip hadn't been in on Soapy's plans, but he knew instantly that Soapy was playing the part of Santa Claus.

"Soapy!" Speed yelled.

"Quiet!" Chip urged. "It looks as if Santa's got some gifts for someone."

Then Santa Claus handed beautifully wrapped gifts to each of the little girls and to Mrs. Phillips too. He gave them each a kiss on the cheek and then walked over in front of Speed. Santa placed a State University lollipop the size of a basketball in the speedster's hand. "Little boys should be seen and not heard, sonny," he said, patting Speed on the head. "Stick that in your mouth!"

Then Soapy pulled off the mask. "Let's eat!" he said happily. "I'm starved!"

"You're always starved!" Speed gibed.

Mrs. Phillips came to the head of the table and they all sat down to their Christmas meal. "Please bow your heads with me," she said. "Thank you, God, for the tremendous miracle these many people brought to us. Please bless this day and this food, and may all people feel your peace this special Christmas Day. Amen."

What a feast! The table was laden with food. Mrs. Phillips had supervised the preparations, but Pete and Jimmy had done the actual cooking. Just to make sure there was enough for everyone, Pete had made two trips into town with the truck to raid his restaurant. They finished up with pumpkin pie, ice cream, milk, and big slices of fruitcake. Soapy put up a good fight and tried to eat everything in sight, but he finally had to quit. With relish, he whipped off his black Santa Claus belt and let out a great sigh. "I'm stuffed!"

The guests all thanked Mrs. Phillips, Pete, and Jimmy and then Paddy Clark rose to his feet and asked if he might say something. The crew quieted, and the timberman walked up to Mrs. Phillips at the head of the table.

"This is the greatest Christmas dinner I've ever attended," Clark said, patting his stomach. "And the most unusual. I wouldn't have missed it for the world." He paused and pulled an envelope out of his pocket. "Mrs. Phillips," he said, "as the representative of all your guests, I want to present you with this envelope. It contains a check in payment for the logs and stumpage and—" He paused for a moment, taming his emotions, and then continued. "And it's big enough to fix up your house and to send Branch back to school and back to basketball!"

The guests cheered and yelled and pounded the table for all they were worth.

"Frankly," Clark continued, "I never thought Chip and Branch and you fellas could swing the job. But I should have known better than to underestimate a group of State University athletes. Personally," he said earnestly, "all my life I will remember the opportunity you gave me to be a part of this wonderful gesture. I wish I could have done more."

Clark looked briefly at Chip. "In fact, I even talked to George Grayson about that, but he said it would ruin everything. Now, knowing what I do and seeing what I've seen, I quite agree. You fellows did the whole thing yourselves. And you didn't ask for help. You had confidence in your ability to do it and you never gave up. I'm sure you realize that you got more out of this experience than money can buy. Congratulations!"

Holding the envelope in her hands, Mrs. Phillips got slowly to her feet. Every person in the room stood and applauded. There were tears in the eyes of a lot of the timbermen when they sat down.

For a moment, Mrs. Phillips was speechless. She took a deep breath and looked around the room, focusing her eyes briefly on each boy. Then she began to speak.

"Christmas is the most joyous of all days," she said reverently. "This day means much to everyone. It's the day for peace on earth and goodwill toward our fellow men. Surely God has brought you all here today. And I am sure that no one has ever experienced a greater Christmas than *I* have today. Your kindness and generosity take me back to the days of my youth. To the days when the neighbors of a community joined together to build a house or a barn or to help harvest the crops for those who were in need."

There were tears in her eyes and her voice broke. After a brief moment she continued. "I thought everyone had forgotten that sort of thing—that today, people are so wrapped up in their own lives that there was no room left to give thought to the problems of others. But I was wrong!

"It took you fine boys to prove just how wrong. Branch and the girls and I want to thank all of you—especially Chip Hilton and Soapy Smith and Mr. Pete Thorpe and Jimmy Chung and you, Mr. Paddy Clark, and Coach Corrigan and his friends—from the bottoms of our hearts. And may God bless you all."

CHAPTER 19

Last Team Clasp

"WE'LL KILL 'EM," Soapy said aggressively. He thrust his red and blue State University bag forward to make a path through the crowd and charged ahead as if he were going to put his words into immediate action.

Branch and Speed hurried behind him, almost running to keep pace with Soapy, and Chip tried to follow. But the opening had disappeared and there was no way through the crowd. So he followed the chattering men, women, and students who were striding briskly along. It wasn't the chilly weather that propelled their pace, and it wasn't the time. It was excitement! The very air was charged with it, almost crackling with its intensity as the fans neared their destination.

Up ahead, Chip could see the marquee of Madison Square Garden with the big lighted letters in the top line spelling out: CHRISTMAS INVITATIONAL TOURNA-MENT, and in smaller letters below: State vs. Wilson University and Northern vs. Southwestern.

Chip saw that he wasn't going to catch up with his friends. He glanced at his watch to make sure it was only seven o'clock. Then he resigned himself to going it alone. The past three days seemed like a dream, he was thinking. That is, with the exception of last night. He wished he could forget Northern State!

His thoughts flashed back to Monday and the Statesmen's arrival at JFK Airport and their bus ride to the hotel. It was his first trip to New York, and the tall buildings, congested streets, and thousands and thousands of people rushing here and there and everywhere had thrilled him. And he had so looked forward to the afternoon practice in Madison Square Garden.

Standing on the court and looking around at the thousands of empty seats and gazing up at the great array of clocks that kept time for world-renowned hockey games, boxing matches, and basketball games, Chip's chest filled with awe. He was still enthralled in the spirit of the dream, with all its marvel.

Then there was Broadway! Chip marveled at the speeding traffic that raced up to a crossing, drew to a fast and brief stop, and then raced away without provoking even a lifted eyebrow from anyone. Chip gazed in amazement at the throngs of people and the dazzling theater lights and brilliant advertising signs that flamed into sight, blacked out, and flamed back again.

And what about Soapy! Chip had delighted in the redhead's complete abandonment in sopping up all the sounds and smells and lights and voices and cries and laughter; he was living it up, fascinated by the turbulence and speeding pulse of this great metropolitan amusement center.

Then there were the headlines and the pages upon pages of sports stories calling the Statesmen the "Cinderella Kids." On TV there were even stories of their experiences as timbermen and their devotion to a fellow teammate. The pictures of the Phillips farm and the Christmas dinner somehow found their way into the New York papers. And then there were the write-ups listing Chip's scoring records and accomplishments.

LAST TEAM CLASP

But the Garden! At night! It was the sports center of the world, the culmination of months of anticipation for Chip and his team. Endless lines of fans—who somehow miraculously found their way through the labyrinth of corridors, stairs, and escalators to the right seats—were just as eager. The thrill of excitement at the sight of the teams dashing out on the floor brought a roar from onlookers. Then the tumult began, and the shouting grew in intensity until the official tossed up the first ball of the game. The action grew more furious with each minute of play until someone won and someone lost.

State's bye as defending champions had given the team a much-needed rest. Then came the big moment for Chip and for the Statesmen, the moment when they ran out on the floor for their first game. The acclaim of the fans and the introductions, with each player receiving a big round of applause one by one when his name was called, were amazing.

There was the exhilaration of victory! It was a great win for the Statesmen. Although they had played sloppily and poorly, they had managed to squeeze out a victory over Templeton by a single point: 71-70. And the dream had begun to come true!

There was the thrill of being photographed before, during, and after the games by the big-time photographers. The talks with the basketball writers from the great metropolitan newspapers. The column-long write-ups about Chip's point race with Kinser of Southwestern for top-scoring honors of the nation.

But then, in the semifinals, the end of the dream stopped it all. Suddenly, irrevocably and conclusively, they had lost to Northern State by two points, 83-81.

Tonight they were nearing the end of the road; they were playing Wilson University in the consolation game as a preliminary to the great championship final between Northern State and mighty Southwestern.

Wilson University brought back memories of State's first game of the season. That night he had sat in the stands with Branch Phillips and watched Henninger, the great Wilson center, dominate the boards and lead his teammates to an easy victory over State, humiliating them with a score of 96-70.

Well, as Soapy had said, it would be different tonight. It had to be different! There *was* no tomorrow for this dream.

Chip presented his pass to the doorman, hurried through the door, and walked along in the soft light of the great corridor until he came to dressing room number 12. Andre Gilbert pulled him inside and pointed to a locker. Murph Kelly was taping Dom's ankles, and Coach Corrigan was standing beside the white board. As Chip passed him, Kelly looked up and growled, "Hurry up! You're next."

Chip climbed on the table and once more his thoughts shot ahead to the game. Then Kelly smacked his leg, Chip hopped down, and Jimmy took his place for taping. Chip sat down between Soapy and Branch and got into his uniform. Branch was fussing nervously with his locker, and Soapy was telling Speed about one of his experiences on Broadway. By the time Chip had laced up his shoes, everyone was dressed.

Then someone knocked on the door and shouted: "Seven-thirty. You're due on the floor in ten minutes!"

"Heads up!" Corrigan said, clearing his throat and walking in front of the team. He pointed to the match-ups on the white board. "Same crew we played before," he said shortly, his words tumbling one after another. "It's another big team—same style of play. Tough on the boards! In better shape than we are and fighting mad.

"Last night, as you know, they lost by three points to Southwestern, the tourney favorite. So they're all steamed up. And they are remembering the beating they gave us a month ago on our own court, so they're figuring on running us right out of Madison Square Garden.

"But we lost a close one last night too. And *we're* steamed up. Northern State beat us, but they were lucky. Lucky we weren't in shape!

"We've got a lot of things going for us tonight. We've loosened up a bit, and the best shot in basketball began to get his eye on the basket last night. We've got a big man starting for us tonight who thinks every player on this squad is the greatest guy who ever picked up a basketball . . . and he's right!

"Besides, there's a bunch of hard-nose football guys back in University who put on basketball shoes and risked their necks to prove what they thought of their school and the players on this team. That's ammunition enough right there to beat Wilson University, Southwestern, and Northern State all in one night. So, men, let's go!"

Corrigan's hand shot out, and Chip and his teammates scrambled off the benches and crowded around him. Chip wanted to make sure he got in on *this* team clasp, the last one he would ever share with Corrigan, at least as a college player.

The Garden was swarming with fans when the Statesmen ran out on the court, and there were only a few empty seats in the huge arena by the time they finished with their warm-up drill. Along one side of the court, sports writers from New York and all over the country were sitting behind the press tables, already tapping away on their laptops. At the far end of the long row, Chip glimpsed Bill Bell. The *Herald* sports editor caught Chip's eye. He smiled and shook his fist in a gesture of "fight." Chip smiled in return and nodded.

Chip knew he was "on" with the first shot he took in the warm-up drill. And he felt a surge of confidence when he noted that his teammates' passes and shots were also sharp and true. Then the game buzzer sounded, and they gathered around Corrigan in front of the State bench. Coach Corrigan sent him out to the center circle to shake hands with Tom

Jones, the Wilson University captain. Jones was six-seven, and Chip had to look up at the player against whom Corrigan had matched him.

The referee ran through the usual game instructions, and then Chip walked swiftly back to join his teammates. Seconds later they were lined up for the center tap. Dom gave the signal for a back tap, and Henninger and Branch went up high in the air. The ball came back to Chip straight and true, and he grinned in relief. Branch had taken the tap away from Henninger. It was a good start!

Chip dribbled slowly forward into the front court, then put on a burst of speed and drove around his tall opponent to score with a jumper in the lane.

Wilson brought the ball down and went into its possession formation to give Henninger a chance to get a good pivot position near the basket. But Branch was on him and stayed there, keeping between the powerful player and the ball. Wilson couldn't get the ball in to the pivot. After several passes, Murray, Wilson's backcourt quarterback, leaped high above Jimmy and tried a jumper from the circle. But the shot was off line, and the ball bounced high above the basket.

Right then, Branch gave the fans something to cheer about. His elbows were even with the hoop when he grabbed the ball. Then, while he was still in the air, he twisted around and fired the ball to Jimmy. Jimmy dribbled swiftly into the center of the court and continued to the State free-throw line. Chip cut down the left sideline, and Bitsy sped down the right. Jimmy faked a shot to draw one of the Wilson guards toward him and then hit Chip with the ball. Chip laid it against the board for two more points. State led 4-0.

The Engineers came down and scored on a long three-pointer by Grant, but in one long step, Branch grabbed the ball out of the net and landed out of bounds. Then he whipped the ball to Bitsy, who was speeding up the sideline.

Bitsy passed to Jimmy, and the uncanny dribbler fed the ball to Chip under the basket for another score.

The Statesmen had their running game going now, and Wilson tried the same type of play. But the Engineers lacked the speed and finesse of the Statesmen; they were too tall for the lightning passes and hard running, and their big men couldn't keep up with Jimmy, Bitsy, and Chip. They fell ten points behind before the Wilson captain called for a time-out.

Chip wanted to keep loose, so he moved restlessly from one foot to the other as he stood in front of the bench. And over and over again he could hear a group of fans shouting: "Break the record! Break the record!" When the Wilson Engineers came back from their huddle with their coach, they went back to their possession game and concentrated on stopping State's fast break. But State still led by nine points at the end of the third quarter. During the time-out, Chip heard a group in the crowd chanting: "Seventy-one! Seventy-one! Break the record!" The players' tired muscles were rebelling now, and the State attack began to stall. Corrigan called for a time-out and they walked wearily toward the sideline. The players on the bench made them sit down to rest, and when time was up, Corrigan took another time-out.

Now Chip could hear voices from the crowd calling his name again, rooting for him to break the Garden's collegiate scoring record. "Come on, Hilton. Break the record! Come on! Shoot!"

When the playing resumed, Wilson played careful ball and slowly closed the gap. Chip was carrying the brunt of the State scoring now, and the chant of the crowd became a roar.

"Shoot, Hilton! Shoot!"

He scored a long three-pointer and was fouled in the process of shooting. The crowd went wild. He made the free throw, and the roar continued on and on.

Wilson came right back and scored. The Engineers scored again and caught up and passed the weary Statesmen to lead, 96-95, with a minute left to play.

Corrigan used his last time-out. When the players circled him, he pleaded with them to let Chip or Jimmy try for the score. "Don't hold the ball," he said. "We've got to score. Let Chip or Jimmy take the shot!"

The pressure was on now, and the fans in the Garden were on their feet. Jimmy took the ball out of bounds and passed in to Bitsy. The little guy brought the ball upcourt and passed back to Jimmy. Jimmy swiftly caught Obert off balance and drove in for a layup, but Henninger blocked the shot, and Obert recovered the ball. Now it was a battle of nerves.

Chip looked at the clock. Only fifty seconds!

State was in a full-court press, but the Engineers got safely past the ten-second line and began to freeze the ball.

Thirty seconds. Twenty-five! Twenty!

The crowd roar increased as the clock ticked away the seconds. It was now or never for the Statesmen. Chip and his teammates were playing their hearts out, calling on their last bit of strength to leech their opponents. Murray was putting on a deadly dribble freeze now, teasing Jimmy as he deftly maneuvered back and forth across the court. Jimmy pressed closer and closer, dogging the Wilson star, sticking to him as if he were the dribbler's shadow.

Chip was concentrating on Jones, but he heard Soapy yelling, "Get the ball! Get the ball!"

Then Jimmy made his move. He sprang forward with a desperate do-or-die leap, and his eager fingertips got a piece of the ball and deflected it to the side. He continued his dive, ending up on the floor. But he had the ball!

Chip had seen the play coming and had sprinted past Jones and dashed for the State basket. Without looking, Jimmy threw the ball far back over his head, and Chip caught it at a dead run. He dribbled for the basket with Jones hard on his heels.

He could have forced the shot and possibly could have made it. But he saw Branch tearing for the basket from the other side of the court and, without the slightest hesitation, bounced the ball to his teammate. Branch gathered the precious ball in without breaking stride, went up for the shot, and was just releasing it when Henninger caught up to him and knocked the ball out of bounds. But the big Engineer couldn't stop; he crashed into Branch, and the two of them ended up on the floor.

The referee blasted his whistle just before the buzzer sounded and pointed toward Henninger. "Two!" he yelled. "Two shots!"

Then, with twenty thousand delirious fans standing, applauding, stamping, yelling, and cheering, and with the game over as far as regulation time was concerned, Branch stepped slowly up to the line. He bounced the ball once and then flipped it up and out. It went spinning down through the hoop to tie the score!

The referee retrieved the ball, tossed it to Branch, and moved out of the lane. Once again, Branch stepped up to the line. Chip was standing on the lane next to Jones, straining in toward the big opponent, every ounce of his being at the breaking point. Branch bounced the ball twice and then jiggled it in his hands. Taking aim at the basket, he lifted his arms and let the ball go. The ball went spinning, up and out and straight and true, and fell cleanly through the basket to break the tie and win the consolation game for the Statesmen. They had done it!

CHAPTER 20

The Real Purpose of Sports

ALL AROUND CHIP camera flashes and TV camera lights blinded him. Reporters, teammates, Wilson players, officials, and fans were crowding around him, shaking his hand, patting him on the back, raving and ranting about a new all-time Garden record. Then the questions: How did it feel to score seventy-three points in a game? Wasn't he afraid Phillips would miss the two free throws, since this was the big player's first big tournament game? Did he know that he was a cinch to win the tournament's most valuable player award?

They followed him off the court and blocked his path when he got to the corridor under the side arena. More and more fans continued to press forward and thread their way through the mob so they could get close to him and touch him, pat him on the back, shake his hand, and ask for his autograph.

It took him ten minutes to get to locker room number 12. He could hear his teammates yelling and throwing things, and then Andre Gilbert peeked out and opened the door wide enough to let him inside. Branch and Jimmy were standing up on the trainers' table, and they yelled and pointed toward him as the mad celebration started all over again.

The players rushed him and heaved him up between Branch and Jimmy. Soapy was yelling something about killing all the rest of their opponents piece by piece, and the guys were hollering for Branch to make a speech. The big guy was grinning and trying to control his feelings, but tears were streaming down his cheeks, and he couldn't have said anything right then even if he'd wanted to.

Then good old Soapy—reliable, effervescent, and persistent creator of commotion, turmoil, and trouble—stepped diplomatically into the ring and began bellowing that Coach Corrigan wanted to say something.

Then Corrigan got the treatment. Dom and Rudy grabbed him and hoisted him up on the table. The players gave their young coach half a dozen cheers before they would let him say a word. When they quieted, Jim Corrigan began to talk. It was a sentimental speech and much of it could have been due to the excitement of the moment, but one could tell it came from his heart.

"Men" he began, "it was a fine win. You're a great team. I'm proud of you—"

"We wanted to win the tournament for you, Coach," Chip said.

Corrigan nodded understandingly. "I knew that, and I appreciate it with all my heart. But there's more to coaching than winning games and championships and medals and cups and trophies. There's loyalty to school and team and teammates. Cups tarnish and championships are forgotten every time a new champion appears.

"But the true friendship and spirit of sacrifice and team play that you men possess will be with you always. As for myself, working with you and with your captain has been an inspiration. And the memory of what you did to help your school and a teammate in his time of need will be with me always. I will never forget how you sacrificed to help a good friend. And I'll never forget how you fought your hearts out when your muscles were sore and torn and as tight as the strings of a piano. Nor will I forget the sight of your hands that look as if they've been grabbed off a butcher's meat block.

"Now, since you are all leaving directly from New York to go on to your homes, this must be my good-bye to you and my good-bye to basketball too. At least for a while. I want you to know that I feel I am the luckiest coach in the world. I was fortunate to have had the privilege of working with a bunch of athletes who proved they know the real purpose of sports.

"I'm sure all of you know the little verse Grantland Rice wrote—

'When the One Great Scorer comes
To mark against your name,
He writes not that you won or lost—
But how you played the game.'"

Corrigan paused and looked at each of them in turn. Then he continued: "When Grantland Rice wrote that, I'm sure he was thinking about athletes just like you. Just like you, Chip. And like you, Jimmy, Dom, Bitsy, Rudy, Speed, Branch, J. C., Bill, Rick, Marty, Bo, and, last but not least—like you, Soapy Smith.

"Now I'll have to take a leaf out of Soapy's book and say that I know—just as surely as I know I am standing here in a Madison Square Garden locker room—that come next March, Chip will be the nation's top scorer and captain of the NCAA national champions. And you'll kill 'em!"

• • •

STATE UNIVERSITY'S basketball team, sparked by Chip Hilton, seems headed for another victorious season. Then, in midseason, a new coach, with an entirely different system of play, takes over. In rapid succession, a series of events puts the brakes on State's high hopes. Everyone who enjoys basketball and swift action will welcome *Buzzer Basket,* the next exciting basketball story in Coach Clair Bee's Chip Hilton Sports series.

Afterword

Sportsmanship means fair play.
It means having respect for the other person's point of view.
It means a real application of the Golden Rule.
Fair play and sportsmanship, if practiced,
will go a long way in developing a finer type
of citizenship throughout the country.
Knute Rockne, 1925

KNUTE ROCKNE and Clair Bee will be remembered forever as two of the greatest coaches of all time. Both won recognition because of their amazing records and because of their innovative approaches to their sports. Both made lesser-known but no less lasting contributions to our understanding of how sports participation can foster character development.

Rockne coached at a time when the value of collegiate sports was very much in question. He had to make a case for why colleges, including Notre Dame, should support football programs. He argued in the leading newspapers and journals of his day for football's value, not as entertainment or as a marketing tool, but for football's value as a powerful means of civic and character education.

Sports, like the rest of our social life, depend upon a commitment to fairness, and fairness, as Rockne noted, entails respect and "a real application of the Golden Rule." The enjoyment of any competitive game depends on the worthiness of one's opponent. To rise to the challenge presented by an opponent, whose skills and determination match or surpass our own, is to stretch our capacities to the fullest. The result can be some of the most exhilarating moments in a lifetime.

Clair Bee, like Knute Rockne, understood the fundamental importance of fair play and respect. Clair Bee never questioned whether sports could build character. In the Chip Hilton Sports Series, he showed again and again how respect, empathy, and fairness are essential threads in the fabric of sports participation.

I grew up reading and rereading Chip Hilton books. Through them, Clair Bee nourished in me a love of reading and a love of sports for which I am deeply grateful. My love of reading led me over many years to become a university professor in Notre Dame's Great Books Department, the Program of Liberal Studies. My love of sports led me and my colleagues, Brenda Bredemeier and David Shields, to establish the Mendelson Center for Sport, Character, and Culture at Notre Dame, a center devoted to fostering character development through youth sports.

Unlike many of those who have written forewords and afterwords for the Chip Hilton series, I never became a sports hero or even a varsity athlete. Yet sports played a crucial role in my upbringing. Even before I could read, I began each day with the sports page propped between the corn flakes box and my cereal bowl, reviewing the latest scores and standings with my dad. I was the first kid to show up after school at the sandlot and the basketball court in the school parking lot and the last one to race home for dinner. In high school and college, I never missed a home game. As a parent, I coached girls and boys between the ages of seven and fourteen in three different sports. To this day, I play regularly in pickup lunchtime basketball games.

I have spent most of my professional life studying social development and moral education. In the last several years, I have turned my attention to the tremendous educational potential of youth sports. I say potential because not all children have the positive sports experiences that Chip Hilton had. Coaches and fans sometimes lose sight of why children play sports in the first place. They forget that children play sports to have fun and that sports are, after all, simply games.

When I was growing up, we organized our own games. We were our own coaches and referees. We chose fair teams, designed our plays, and called our own fouls. We became accomplished arbitrators and counselors. We understood that unless everyone went home having had fun, there wouldn't be enough players for a game the next day. Over the last forty years, organized youth sports have progressively replaced the pickup games of my childhood. Adults have taken over the leadership roles once played by children, roles psychologists see as vital to social and moral development.

We began the center at Notre Dame because we were concerned about this transition. We need to find ways to give sports back to children. This does not mean that adults should abandon youth sports programs. It does mean, however, that we need to provide children with safe playgrounds and opportunities to have their own pickup games. When we do involve children in organized sports, we need to allow them to participate in meaningful ways that can contribute to the development of their character.

I can think of no better guide for youth sports reform than the models of coaching and mentoring offered in the

Chip Hilton series. I am deeply honored to be associated with this series of books that I have so loved. We all owe a debt to Randy and Cindy Bee Farley for introducing the Chip Hilton books to a new generation.

Clark Power
Program of Liberal Studies
Mendelson Center for Sport, Character, and Culture
University of Notre Dame

Your Score Card

I have read: I expect to read:

____ ____ 1. ***Touchdown Pass:*** The first story in the series introduces readers to William "Chip" Hilton and all his friends at Valley Falls High during an exciting football season.

____ ____ 2. ***Championship Ball:*** With a broken ankle and an unquenchable spirit, Chip wins the state basketball championship and an even greater victory over himself.

____ ____ 3. ***Strike Three!:*** In the hour of his team's greatest need, Chip Hilton takes to the mound and puts the Big Reds in line for all-state honors.

____ ____ 4. ***Clutch Hitter!:*** Chip's summer job at Mansfield Steel Company gives him a chance to play baseball on the famous Steelers team where he uses his head as well as his war club.

____ ____ 5. ***A Pass and a Prayer:*** Chip's last football season is a real challenge as conditions for the Big Reds deteriorate. Somehow he must keep them together for their coach.

BACKCOURT ACE

I have   I expect
read: to read:

____   ____   6. ***Hoop Crazy:*** When three-point fever spreads to the Valley Falls basketball varsity, Chip Hilton has to do something, and fast!

____   ____   7. ***Pitchers' Duel:*** Valley Falls participates in the state baseball tournament, and Chip Hilton pitches in a nineteen-inning struggle fans will long remember. The Big Reds' year-end banquet isn't to be missed!

____   ____   8. ***Dugout Jinx:*** Chip is graduated and has one more high school game before beginning a summer internship with a minor-league team during its battle for the league pennant.

____   ____   9. ***Freshman Quarterback:*** Early autumn finds Chip Hilton and four of his Valley Falls friends at Camp Sundown, the temporary site of State University's freshman and varsity football teams. Join them in Jefferson Hall to share successes, disappointments, and pranks.

____   ____   10.***Backboard Fever:*** It's nonstop basketball excitement! Chip and Mary Hilton face a personal crisis. The Bollingers discover what it means to be a family, but not until tragedy strikes.

____   ____   11.***Fence Busters:*** Can the famous freshman baseball team live up to the sportswriter's nickname, or will it fold? Will big egos and an injury to Chip Hilton divide the team? Can a beanball straighten out an errant player?

____   ____   12.***Ten Seconds to Play!:*** When Chip Hilton accepts a job as a counselor at Camp All-America, the last thing he expects to run into is a football problem. The appearance of a junior receiver at State University causes Coach Curly Ralston a surprise football problem too.

____   ____   13.***Fourth Down Showdown:*** Should Chip and his fellow sophomore stars be suspended from the State University football team? Is there a good reason for their violation? Learn how Chip comes to better understand the value of friendship.

YOUR SCORE CARD

BACKCOURT ACE

I have   I expect
read: to read:

____   ____   **19.Backcourt Ace:** The State University basket-
                    ball team has a real height problem, and the solu-
                    tion may lie in seven-footer Branch Phillips. But
                    there are complications. Be sure to read how Chip
                    Hilton and his friends combine ingenuity and self-
                    less service to solve a family's and the team's
                    problems.

About the Author

CLAIR BEE, who coached football, baseball, and basketball at the collegiate level, is considered one of the greatest basketball coaches of all time—both collegiate and professional. His winning percentage, 82.6, ranks first overall among any major college coaches, past or present. His name lives on forever in numerous halls of fame. The Coach Clair Bee and Chip Hilton awards are presented annually at the Basketball Hall of Fame, honoring NCAA Division I college coaches and players for their commitment to education, personal character, and service to others on and off the court. Bee is the author of the twenty-three-volume, best-selling Chip Hilton Sports series, which has influenced many sports and literary notables, including best-selling author John Grisham.